The Between People

Kitty Manning

Attic Press
Dublin

First Published in 1990 by
Attic Press
44 East Essex Street
Dublin 2

British Library Cataloguing in Publication Data
Manning, Kitty
    The between people.
    I. Title
    823.914 [F]

    ISBN 1-85594-012-4

Cover Design: Luly Mason
Origination: Attic Press
Printing: The Guernsey Press Company Ltd.

Although the place names in this book refer to real places, the characters are entirely fictional.

This book is published with the assistance of The Arts Council / An Chomhairle Ealaíon.

About the Author

Born in England of Irish parents, when she was five years old Kitty Manning moved to Northern Ireland where most of her family still live. In the early 1960s she moved to Dublin, has five children and works in hospital administration.

Acknowledgements

Thanks to my mother, Catherine O'Reilly, for her encouragment; to my husband and family for their patience; to Sean McCann, former Features Editor of the *Evening Press*, who gave me my first chance.

THE PRESENT

Two women walked up a steep wide hill away from the town below.

Although in each other's company, they walked too far apart for conversation, the older woman concentrating her energy on the climb before her, the younger woman gazing around her as she walked along. When they came to a slight level spot in the middle of the hill they stopped at the same instant - where they had always stopped in the past when they lived in this area - and stood for a moment resting. The younger woman walked over to the other.

"Is the climb too much for you, Mother? I should have brought the car."

"No, I'll be alright." Harriet Regan stood panting, her hand lightly resting on her chest. "I wanted to see if I could still climb this hill after all these years and if it was as steep as I remembered it."

"And is it?"

"Steeper I would say but then I'm older. Still we're nearly halfway up now - we'll keep going. Look how near we are to the old Cathedral."

The wide street led up to the gates of the ancient church high above the town. As they looked they saw the figure of a woman emerge from the narrow street which ran to the left of the Church and was just outside its perimeter wall. They stared towards her - the first person they had seen since they began to climb the hill.

"Look daughter, look up thonder," said Harriet dropping into the local dialect as she neared the top of the street. "That's Shirley Cummins coming towards us, you know the wee gawk who used to work in the shop across the street from our house."

"But Shirley Cummins was young. Thone's a wee fat woman," said her daughter Kate, answering in kind.

"Don't forget it's a long time since we lived here. It's her alright, I'd know those bandy legs anywhere, you could wheel a horse and cart through them."

The woman stared curiously towards them as she approached, she hesitated for a moment and then came over.

"Aren't you Mrs Regan?" she said touching Kate on the arm. She looked towards the older woman, a puzzled expression on her face.

"No, you are Mrs Regan, you must be Kate. Haven't you grown very like your mother - not that you've changed much yourself, missus," she said, walking over to Harriet and staring at what the years had done to her.

"Well, it is you Shirley. I thought it was you coming along. You haven't changed a bit. So you're still working in the shop in King Street?"

"There's no wee shop in King Street and nobody lives there now, not since it was bombed. I go up and walk around it sometimes, I miss it you know."

"Bombed?"

They stared at her. Who would want to bomb a ramshackle place like King Street?

"Aye, the troubles have been bad here since you left, a huge car bomb blew the place to smithereens. Now that I remember, it was planted right outside your front door - where yez used to live, that is."

King Street gone. Kate felt sick.

"Who would do a thing like that?"

"It was never claimed." It sounded like an unwanted prize in a raffle. "Some people say it was the Provos, because of the Brits going to the dance hall down the street and drinking in the pub."

"British soldiers always drank in the pub and went to the dances."

Kate fell silent, her eyes far away, remembering.

"If the IRA wanted to get them, why would they use a car bomb and blow the whole street apart? Why not put a bomb in the bar and a separate one in the hall?"

"That's what we think, it doesn't make sense," said Shirley missing the irony of Harriet's remark. "It was more likely to have been some of them oul' Protestant paramilitaries bombing the street out of badness - because of all the Catholics living in it."

Kate saw Harriet's face close in annoyance.

Shirley has forgotten that my mother was once a Protestant, she thought.

"I'm surprised you didn't read about it in the newspapers Mrs Regan."

"The only things that I read are the death notices - the only news in the papers nowadays is bad news. Kate lives in England. She doesn't see the Irish papers."

"We had reporters here from England after the bomb - not that we wanted them. They went snooping around, asking questions, catching people unawares while their flashbulbs went off. The streetdwellers were taken to the old people's home after the bombing. They were very upset when they saw themselves in the paper the following day, with their bits and pieces gathered around them and the shells of their homes behind them. You know how dignified they always were."

Harriet threw a look towards Kate. She never remembered them as being dignified.

"Poor Annie Greene had left her teeth in a cup beside her pillow when she went to bed that night and there she was on the front page of the paper with her mouth clapped in around shrivelled gums, she had become an oul' doll overnight. Then Mr McKeown, you know yourselves that he had never been seen without his brown hat - he even sat down to Sunday dinner wearing it - well he appeared in one of them colour magazines in the Sunday papers. Poor oul' divil, he never recovered from the shame of it. He had a huge dome of a head and it was a queer white colour, like the underbelly of a herring. Somehow he looked - exposed." Her chins quivered with emotion.

Kate listened with fascination while the gossip went on - remembering how she used to stand on the concrete floor of the wee shop, dwarfed by the high counter, eavesdropping on the conversations that Shirley had with her customers. But Shirley, after she had given what she considered to be her fair share of information, was now asking questions, expecting a just return for her labour.

"We heard you went to live somewhere up in Antrim," she said to Harriet, "You left the street without a word of goodbye ..."

"She went to live with her brother Billy in Ballymena," Kate answered.

Shirley froze, her nose twitched. So she had gone back to her own. Yes, she had heard that one of them lived in Ballymena. This was news indeed. Harriet had begun to retreat by taking small backward steps that distanced her from Shirley. She nodded a sharp command towards her daughter to join her but Shirley was determined not to give up her source of news easily. She folded her arms and leaned forward to an invisible counter. The bow of her legs seemed to widen slightly to accommodate the redistributed weight of her body.

"Didn't you go to the nursing?" she said to Kate "We always thought you wouldn't be able for it after you having consumption and all. I mind the time you used to sit for hours looking out through your bedroom windows. We used to see your wee white face from the shop across. There were two windows in your room and you were always looking through one or the other."

"Yes," Kate said. "The Catholic window and the Protestant window."

The two women stared at her. She shrugged and looked embarrassed.

"That's the way that I used to think of them. One looked out onto the Catholic Cathedral, one looked out onto the Protestant one."

"That was the year before you went away wasn't it? Still you must have got over your illness alright. I suppose you're married to some Englishman?"

"I'm not married."

Kate saw something like pity in the other woman's eyes.

I have been married and I don't live alone now, she wanted to say, but she knew her situation could never be explained to anyone from King Street. 'Living in sin', Shirley would call it, and as Kate approached the old street and the past, the guilt which had always dogged her then began to descend on her like a cloak.

"I didn't stick with nursing," she added. "I left it and went to work for a newspaper."

She saw shock register, and Shirley's hand went up to guard her mouth. She bid them a polite farewell choosing her words carefully - in case they might appear in print - and hurried down the hill.

"That got rid of her fairly sharp," Harriet said, looking after the retreating figure. She turned on Kate, her face grey and strained.

"What were you doing clattering and talking to her, telling her all our business?"

"I wasn't telling her anything," Kate said, stung by her mother's remark. "I was being civil to someone we used to know."

"What do you mean we used to know her? We always kept to ourselves. Do you think that her and

14

her cronies were ever nice to me? They never forgot for one minute that my father was Tom Menary."

They walked a little way, then once again Harriet had to stop to catch her breath. Kate moved closer to her but she could feel her mother move away slightly when she went to take her arm.

"Mother, it was all a long time ago. Look, we're almost there."

They started off again, walking slowly now; soon they stood at the top of the hill and stopped to regain their breath. Like people who have scaled a mountain they turned to look back down and marvel at how well they had negotiated the almost perpendicular hill. Their lungs were filled with oxygen, their heads with a feeling of euphoria.

They looked towards each other, then together they turned and walked into King Street.

* * *

Nothing Shirley had said had prepared Kate for the reality of King Street. It had disappeared. She had pictured a bombed site, derelict houses, boarded windows, obscenely exposed bedrooms. What she saw was an old road running through open country in the form of a rippling meadow, overgrown with poppies, thousands of them, drifting scarlet on a cloth of gold. What was once a narrow street of uneven grey houses was now a riot of colour. Kate's heart soared with delight as she gazed around. She wanted to run across this dancing meadow, spread invisible wings, soar into the azure sky above. As she looked closer she could see reminders of the past and the terrible thing that had happened here. On the borders of the grassland were heaps of rubble and twisted metal, camouflaged by nettles and young mintgreen leafy briar. She realized that the bombing had been some time ago but she could almost see the bulldozers that must have come grinding their way up the steep hill to flatten the remains of the houses. Later heavy lorries would have come and carted most of the debris away. Now the place had a pastoral look. She could see distant trees, a horizon, and when she looked up, an endless stretch of sky. Never when she had lived here had she seen more than a patch of blue.

She stood at the edge of the road and felt a stinging sensation at the back of her eyes.

King Street was beautiful for the first time.

"Mother," she whispered, "look at the poppies - they're beautiful."

But Harriet shuddered and backed away.

"They give me the creeps, they grow from corpses. It was always said of this place that it was a burial ground in pagan times, that there were human sacrifices here ..." She shivered again. "No wonder there are so many poppies."

The street ran in a semicircle outside the grounds of the old Cathedral and was in fact church property. They walked along the edge of the road where the footpath used to be, gazing around them mesmerised, bumping into each other as they had always done, stumbling on cement-covered bricks, hidden in the uneven grass. They saw that the wall which bounded the Cathedral was broken and they could see the orchard and the old Protestant graveyard which Kate had once been able to glimpse from her bedroom window. Where had they lived exactly? Here? Or here? Kate stepped back and forward nervously, even now she did not want to trespass on her neighbours' property. Harriet stepped forward, getting her bearings immediately.

"This is where our house was. Look, the old stove was here. Come over and warm your hands."

Kate walked towards her and the two of them stood bending over a scutch of grass, rubbing their hands and laughing. Then, feeling silly, Kate straightened up and walked away.

"Use the mat," her mother called after her, still playing the game. "Don't be carrying muck into the hall on your shoes - I've just polished it."

Kate stood there confused. Surely they hadn't lived in this tiny space where one could almost reach from the hall to the kitchen stove. It had always seemed such a big house, Harriet had always called it a big gloomy barracks of a house. Kate had found it terrifying. It was a house where doors opened for no reason, boards creaked furtively outside bedroom doors, lights failed inexplicably. She remembered high brass door-handles that she couldn't reach, running through long corridors in the dark, high-ceilinged rooms lit by pale moonlight. Now she could see that it all rose from this foundation which seemed to her to be no bigger than the scullery.

If this was the hall, it was directly under her bedroom, under the window at the bottom of the bed where she had sat for so long waiting for Steele. She looked up to check her view, yes, this was the hall. She was facing the same angle of the turret of the old Cathedral, the same trees swayed in the breeze casting a shadow over the stained glass window of the church. But now they were just trees, it was merely an old church looking over the ruins of small houses. She breathed a sigh of relief. Maybe by coming back she had laid the ghost of a past love which had always haunted her. She walked over to her mother.

"Where have all the people gone? The people who lived here?"

Harriet looked at her daughter with old frightened eyes.

"Dead. They're all dead and gone."

"No, that's not possible, they couldn't all be dead."

But you are right, she thought, it's thirty years since we moved in here, you were a young woman and even then they were old.

"And small loss to them," Harriet said, her face reddening with remembered insults, "They were no friends of ours."

"Come on, Mother" Kate said quickly, "We've seen enough. We'll go back down by Dobbin's Lane and have something to eat in May's hotel before we go home."

They walked away from the old Cathedral down the steep hill towards the main street below. King Street was part of an old ring road that circled the Cathedral. There were three roads running down from it to the wider circle of the town below. They had come up by Wellington Street, the widest of these roads, now they were descending by Dobbin's Lane, the narrowest. But even this little lane had changed beyond belief. The whole area was gutted, partly bombed, partly cleared for rebuilding. They walked along, sometimes in single file, on the parts of the narrow footpath that remained.

"Merciful heavens, the Hughes's house has gone."

"I think that must be where the Flynns lived."

"Surely that couldn't be the golf course - it is, there's the Bishop's Palace beside it. I never thought that they were so near."

"We could never see them with the old houses."

"And the smoke from the chimneys."

"There's the old Chapel."

"What's left of it. It was a ruin even in our day."

"There's a ghost there," Kate spoke seriously. She was twelve again.

"Another ghost," Harriet smiled. "I thought I knew them all."

"Yes, a light glows there at night. I used to see it when I was going for the eggs on Saturday nights."

She shivered at a sudden unpleasant memory.

They reached the bottom of the hill and walked back down towards May's hotel. The town looked old and shabby, the people who passed them by seemed small and huddled - they had lived through bad times. Kate saw hostile looks directed towards her. Her clothes were different, she stood out as a stranger. She stared into strange faces, craned her neck towards passing cars - she was looking for one person. Steele. She would only be in this town for a few hours today and she longed to see him. She could not imagine what he would look like after all these years although she knew his black hair must be grey now.

"Are you coming into this hotel or not?" she heard her mother's voice. "Or would you like to spend the rest of the day outside it gawking at everyone who passes by?"

"Sorry."

She followed Harriet into the hotel. They went into

the lounge

"What would you like to drink? Will I order a sherry?"

She saw her mother's face darken.

"You know that I don't drink. We'll have a lemonade."

"A glass of lemonade - for one," Kate said to the waitress. "I'll have a whiskey."

She didn't like whiskey, would have preferred a brandy, a vodka. But she knew that what her mother would once have referred to as 'John Barleycorn' represented all that was evil and she wanted to make a point. When the drinks arrived she saw by the downturn of Harriet's mouth and the quick flash of her eye towards the glass that she had registered her choice but she made no comment. When Kate enquired about a meal the waitress said she would bring them a menu from the diningroom. They sat side by side, too close together, on an small overstuffed couch, Harriet holding her glass of lemonade selfconsciously, a vague polite smile on her face, her feet barely touching the ground. Kate sipped her whiskey, and could not think of anything to say. They were not easy with each other, mother and daughter. In the past they had seldom gone out together.

The waitress came over to them with the menu. Harriet had forgotten her glasses and Kate ordered for both of them. It was too late for lunch and too early for dinner. They ordered from the à la carte menu, a salad for Kate, a mixed grill for Harriet. Holding the menu Kate could see a tremor in her hand. Tension, almost unknown to her in London, was churning her stomach and turning her legs to jelly in this hotel. She took a quick swig of the whiskey to calm herself and saw with surprise that she had almost finished the glass. She drained the last few drops and looking up, saw her mother's eye on her.

Oh God, now she'll say that I drink too much.

Home sweet home.

Were memories disturbing for everybody or was it just Kate who was so damaged by her past? She must try and pull herself together, try to make sure that her mother enjoyed her day out.

"Do you enjoy living in Ballymena with your brother Billy?" She could not call him Uncle, she had never met him; in the past when her mother had spoken of him, which was seldom - she had always referred to him as 'my brother Billy'.

There was no response and when she looked she saw that Harriet was staring at the wall opposite, her hands clasped tightly around the glass.

"I mean, it's nice to be back with your own people."

The silence stretched. Then, when Kate had begun to think that her mother had heard nothing she said, the voice beside her spoke, low and bitter.

"Who says I'm back with them? Billy never bothered much with the rest of the family. He moved to Ballymena years ago. A while back, I met that Nurse Patterson, she'd heard that he'd had a stroke, that he had nobody to look after him. I decided to eat humble pie and write to him ..."

Kate turned around and flinched from the look in the too-honest eyes.

"He needed me, I needed him. It's as simple as that."

* * *

From across the dining room table Kate watched her mother. Sometimes when she was young she had been stunned by Harriet's beauty, her face then had been young and unformed, her eyes bright and full of hope. Now her expression was one of resignation and suffering; there were deep furrows running from nose to mouth, heavy lines drawing down the edges of her lips. I must have helped to form that face, she thought, yet I know nothing of the woman. She brought me up singlehanded from when I was five, yet she never confided in me, never gave me an inkling as to what she thought or felt.

Harriet looked up from her plate, saw her daughter watching her, and selfconsciously touched each side of her mouth with a linen napkin.

"I'm pleased you can stay with me in Ballymena tonight, these hotels are so expensive." She leaned towards Kate, a fellow conspirator, "Wasn't it a great chance to have you over when Billy was in hospital - he'd read the Riot Act if he thought you slept under his roof."

Kate knew that her mother did not intend to hurt her. She was stating a fact, that Billy, like the rest of Harriet's family, would never acknowledge Kate, the child of a papist. It had always been so but she wished her mother had not said it. She lowered her head and the bitter bile of rejection rose in her throat.

From where she sat in the hotel diningroom she faced the large window which looked out onto the main street. There was a constant stream of passers-by, almost everyone looked in through the window as they passed. She knew they could see what she once saw, a whiteness of starched linen, a gleam of silver, rich people dining ...

High on a hill above the town the clock on the Catholic church chimed and tolled the hour.

"Merciful heavens, is that the time?" Harriet said as she had always said in the past when the clock struck. "We'll have to be getting back. I have to let the cat out and feed the dog."

* * *

"I'm glad we went back today," Kate said as she drove back to Ballymena. "I had no idea that I could feel so emotional about the past, how I felt today when I saw the golf-course ..."

"The golf-course?" Kate glanced over, in the growing darkness she could only see the outline of Harriet's face turned towards her but she knew what the expression would be, could imagine the lips curled in the old scornful manner. "How could you feel emotional about the golf-course? You never played golf in your life."

"I didn't mean that," Kate said. "I meant the feeling of inferiority I felt as a child when I used to see them, the Protestants, playing golf on velvet grass while we, the Catholics, lived with backyards, yowling cats, fishheads and chimneys belching black smoke. I know now that it was a social divide more than a religious one but all the Catholics seemed to live in that part of the town or other places like it."

"Well you escaped, you made sure you looked after number one, leaving me to go begging with my pride in my pocket when I was no longer young."

In the darkness Harriet's voice was bitter as cud.

There was a silence. Then she added, "In my day the golf-course was full of weeds and cowdung."

Kate thought of her childhood when she used to kneel on the sill of the high landing window and stick her head through the open-sashed pane to see, over the chimney pots, tiny figures walking on green sward.

There were no cows on the golf-course and no weeds, she thought. It was Camelot.

"You weren't born in Northern Ireland and you left it when you finished school. You couldn't have deep feelings about that place or the people who lived in it."

Kate looked at her mother in amazement. In that town she had run the gamut of her emotions. Never again was she to be so defenceless and vulnerable.

"It was different for me," Harriet said. "I spent most of my life in this town, half as a middle-class Protestant, half as a working-class Catholic. I'll tell you this much, there isn't a ha'p'orth of difference between them. Six of one, half a dozen of the other. I suppose knowing that has always saved me from being biased."

And Steele, Kate thought, saved me.

"Now remind me about these ghosts. I've forgotten most of them. I think they disappeared when the blackout ended."

"You couldn't forget *The Rector*. And what about *The Lady in Black*?"

Kate didn't, of course, mention *Dizzy Sense*.

Dizzy Sense, the evil companion who haunted her childhood dreams. Kate had never mentioned her to a living soul, not even to Ciara who was her best friend. Kate didn't know any obscenities, but *Dizzy*

24

Sense did and at night when Kate slept she wagged a beckoning finger towards her and mouthed them from her perch high in the corner of the room.

* * *

The driveway was a rutted cart track, it led to Billy Menary's house.

Harriet was slumped in her seat asleep, but now she woke with a start, burrowed deep in her handbag and found the front door key. She reached into the back of the car and dragged Kate's overnight bag into the front.

"You brought enough stuff. Are you sure you're only staying the one night?"

Kate thought there was a note of apprehension in her voice.

"I'll be on the ferry from Larne tomorrow."

From the rear of the house there was the rattle of a chain, a dog barked madly, scrabbled on a wooden gate. A sharp word from Harriet brought instant silence. Kate went over to the door and pushed it gently, in the old days country people had left their doors on the snib at night. But times had changed. Harriet opened the door with a proprietary air and went inside, for a second light flooded through a window before a blind was swiftly drawn. Kate felt a reluctance to follow. She had not been invited in when she called that morning. She stepped back and looked at the house where her mother had spent the last five years. Something about its bulk, black in the moonlight, reminded her of King Street. As she went slowly inside the feeling persisted. The kitchen was large with a stone floor, across one wall was a range, there was even a small mahogany table at the window where she knew Harriet would sit and read when the light was fading. She wondered if Harriet got a newspaper every day, the house was isolated and she remembered her saying that Billy had got rid of the car after his stroke. There was no sign of a television or radio in the room and Kate understood now why Harriet had not known of the bombing in King Street. She wondered how her mother got to Mass. Harriet, who was kneeling in front of the range poking the fire vigorously, looked up as though she understood her thoughts and said,

"He doesn't interfere, we came to that agreement. I get up and go to early Mass, either he doesn't know or doesn't choose to ... Now," she climbed stiffly to her feet and drew a kettle forward on the range, where it immediately began to hum, "take off your coat and make yourself at home while I get a bit of food for the dog ... don't be afraid to take a look around. Billy sleeps down here since he had the stroke, he had a bedroom built on and a wee bathroom for himself. Go in and take a look at it."

She saw that her mother was eager to make her feel at home. To please her she went into the old man's bedroom, saw a chaste single bed, a bible on the table beside it. So Billy was religious like the rest of Harriet's family. God-fearing, she thought with bitterness, rich, crawthumping and blinded by hatred. As she passed the bathroom, she looked in and saw, on a low shelf, a thick rubber undersheet, neatly folded, pads, the brand name familiar to her from her nursing days, stacked high in a corner - the paraphernalia of the incontinent. Her hatred melted to pity - poor old bugger. But surely her mother didn't have to ...

She sensed that she was not alone and turned around. Harriet was standing behind her with her finger on the light switch. Her manner was distant - closing Kate out.

"Would you like something to eat?"

"The electric cooker in the corner," Kate stumbled with embarrassment. "It's like the one that I have at home - I'll make us scrambled eggs. Off to bed you go and I'll bring it up."

Harriet looked pleased.

"Well, if you don't mind. If you're making scrambled eggs will you bring me a wee slice of toast? And mind you don't burn it - you always managed to burn the toast," she said with an old woman's capacity of only remembering the unpleasant things in the past.

Kate made the meal and carried it up to her, propping her up on the pillow to eat it.

We're both playing a game, she thought, the dutiful daughter caring for the frail ageing mother.

But that was not their relationship, it was much more deep and complex. Kate was anything but a dutiful daughter, any attempts at caring for her mother had been met with emotional withdrawal a long time ago. She knew too, that for all her frail appearance, Harriet was a strong and independent woman - and watched coldly how she ate with a hearty appetite. When she had finished she cleared the tray away and quickly rinsed the dishes. She came back up to her mother's room and seeing that she was lying down with her eyes closed, she put the light out and drew back the curtains. As she tiptoed to the door she heard her name called,

"Kate."

It was so seldom that her mother had ever said her name that she froze with surprise. Then she turned around away from the glow of the landing light and walked back to the shadows. Harriet was sitting up in bed, her eyes wide and alert.

"Why did you bring me back there today - back to that old street? I'm glad it was blown up, didn't I always say that someone should put a bomb under it?"

"I thought you might want to see it again."

"Since when do you care what I wanted? No, you wanted to go back. Why did you want to back today?" Harriet insisted. "You never came back to the town while I lived there. Even since I came here you never wanted to go back there - you've always met me in Belfast."

Kate sat down on the bed.

"You're right, I did want to go back. You see I'm trying to write a book, a novel set in Northern Ireland. I don't want to write about the troubles because I left the town before that time. No, I wanted to set the story in the old town that I remembered. That's why I went back today, to get the feel of it. I wanted to see the old street just as it was when I grew up in it, but of course I didn't realise it had gone."

"What's the book about? Tell me about it." Harriet's eyes gleamed with excitement.

Kate opened her bag and took her cigarettes out. With a shaking hand she lit one.

"It's a story of division - one small town with two huge cathedrals set on twin hills. Two archbishops live in two palaces. Each cathedral is packed with worshippers. But these people pass each other every

Sunday going to their place of worship and don't greet each other - even on a Christmas morning. They don't see each other at all. It's as if they're divided by glass. A sick young girl lives in a room with two identical windows. One looks onto the Protestant Cathedral, one to the Catholic. She watches the world through a barrier of glass."

"The front bedroom with the two windows - that was your bedroom. Sure nothing ever happened in that room, I don't see how you could write a book about it."

Harriet lay back on her pillows looking tired and disappointed and Kate guessed that she was wishing that she would leave and let her get to sleep. But she had started now and wanted to finish her story, if only to clarify it in her own mind.

"Two women live in this house, one sleeps at the back of the house, one at the front. They are polite to each other but when the young woman reaches out for help or advice the glass is there. It's as if the older woman is unreal, is ..."

"In other words, it's a story of schizophrenia?"

Kate looked at her mother numb with shock. She had forgotten how intelligent she was, how intuitive. She hadn't realised what she was describing. Nor could she say which woman was the victim of the illness. She didn't dare ask Harriet what she thought.

She was yawning now, barely able to stay awake.

"Are there just two characters?"

"No, the girl has visitors, her friends, her doctor."

"Oh yes," her mother said. "Dr Steele."

Kate spoke carefully, her voice expressing just the right amount of casual interest.

"Does he still live there? I suppose you wouldn't

know ..."

"He's dead. Steele is dead."

She thought her mother must have heard her grunt of shock. As if someone had kicked her in the stomach.

But Harriet showed no sign of having heard. She lay back on her pillow, her eyes glazed with thought.

"Aye, he died a good few years back. Mrs Steele died first, she had cancer, poor thing, and he followed soon after. They say he couldn't live without her."

It had never occurred to her that he might be dead, that she would never see him again. And her mother's voice came back to her.

They say he couldn't live without her.

He could live without me, she thought. He could go on living in that town year after year happily growing old with her. Even now she could feel the heartburning jealousy for a woman who died some years ago. She must not let her mother see her face momentarily unmasked, showing pain and bitterness, nor must she give in to the temptation of telling her. When she did not tell her at the time there was no point in confiding in her now. Harriet would want revenge and it was too late for that.

"Did I not write and tell you? I'm sure I wrote, I must have done."

"No, you didn't tell me."

Kate stood up and walked to the window. She stared out at the still night sky. Suddenly she felt that his spirit, gentle and loving, was close beside her, touched her and she was imbued with the sense of peace and happiness she used to feel when he put his arms around her and held her close.

In a moment the illusion of his presence had gone

and she felt a loss so deep and primeval that she almost cried out in pain. The moment passed and she stood there, shaken.

Oh God, did I love him that much? she thought.

Her breath had fogged the window. She wiped a circle in the pane.

"He's pushing up the daisies," she said.

She turned around to see Harriet's shocked face staring at her from the depths of the pillows.

"Well that beats all. That's all you have to say about a man who was so good to you? After you went away he used to drop in to ask about you, to see how you were getting on. But you didn't care - no gratitude. You never once mentioned him in any letter. You never wrote to thank him for all he had done for you - never even sent him a Christmas card. I was ashamed. I tried to explain to him that you were always like that. Cold as ice. Hard as nails."

She stood with her head bowed and let her mother's abuse wash over her. She could not explain that it was Steele she was quoting. "When you're my age, darling, I'll be pushing up the daisies."

* * *

She left her mother's room and walked up the bare attic stairs to her bedroom. It had been a long day, she was tired now - a dull band of pain pressed her forehead. She stood in the dark room looking through the window, listening to unfamiliar animal cries - seeing the outline of the barn across the steading. It wasn't Spring and she knew she had to be wrong but a scent of appleblossom drifted through the window, filled the room.

She shut the window, to shut out the past, then went over to the bed and climbed between stiff white sheets.

"I'll sleep tonight."

And she did, for a while. Then *Dizzy Sense* was there on the wall beside the window. She gyrated slowly, watching Kate, then she began to grin and make obscene gestures. For the first time she came close, loomed large in front of her. Kate dragged herself from layers of sleep and lay shaking. The night was warm and oppressive. She had done her research properly when she came back to delve into the past. Now she could remember how it felt to be sixteen and to be ill and terrified in that bedroom with the two windows. She lay there rigid and waiting. Outside there was silence. Nothing moved. Gradually she began to relax, to doze.

Then they came.

They shuffled towards her, yellow and wizened from the smoking chimneys and the sunless street. They gathered outside her windows, an old malevolent group, standing on the broken footpath, whispering about her with their bloodless lips, condemning her with nodding heads. Cissy Toner waved a crutch threateningly at her while old Mr Lavery shook his walking stick.

She ran backwards and forwards from one bedroom window to the other, drawing blinds, closing curtains and then, with beating heart, retreating into the dark darker darkest corner of her paranoia.

THE PAST

Chapter One

It was a grey house they lived in, Kate and her mother Harriet, grey stone on the outside and a dull greyness within. It seeped into the dark livingroom, spreading from the high wall at the back of the house and the leaden sky above.

Sometimes they were able to ignore it, engrossed in other aspects of their lives the house became like other people's houses, a background. Then at other times they were optimistic about it. They talked of brightening it up, smilingly suggested orange cushions, flowery curtains, a glass door. Sometimes they made a feeble effort, changing the décor with a small tin of paint and a few rolls of wallpaper - but soon, the all-pervasive greyness would spread and absorb the newness. They would look at it and realise they had picked the wrong colour: what had seemed bright was now, they saw, garish; designs which had seemed modern were merely vulgar. It was then they would speak of leaving, covering their despair with mirth. They would win the pools - it seemed totally irrelevant to them that they did not fill in a football coupon - be left a legacy. Sometimes they even thought of an accident, nothing serious, maybe a light fitting falling in a shop and glancing off Kate's shoulder, for accidents she seemed to be the one who was singled out. They read aloud and with envy snippets in the newspapers telling of large settlements for minor injuries. What they could not acknowledge either in their fantasies or in reality was the fact that they were there in that grey house, in that seedy street, in that forgotten town and the odds were that they would remain there for eternity.

The house fronted a dull narrow pot-holed street, a semicircle of ugliness surrounding an old cathedral. Their lives were dominated by the church bell, even though it tolled its message for the Protestant community and they were the Catholic.

"Get up now, that's the eight o'clock bell, you'll be late for Mass."

The town was narrow and humpbacked, arrogant because of its history. It was acknowledged as being the seat of Christianity in their island. The dead were in the streets, old houses carried plaques remembering them. A more sinister dead were with them too, ghosts in bottles cemented into walls, doors sealed never to open, windows covered with black glass blindly proclaimed their story.

Sometimes it seemed to Kate that they had always lived there, the two of them, that they had materialised from some dark and dusty corner of the house, a mother and daughter already fashioned, complete with their weaknesses and their prejudices. At other times they seemed to move around the house, strangers, bumbling into each other, apologising politely, each secretly wondering how she came to be in this strange place with this unknown person, hoping she could soon leave and return to her normal environment.

Harriet Regan was part of the old City, her family was steeped in its history. The monuments in the old graveyard across arose from the bones of her ancestors, most of the old buildings bore some mark of their trade. But Harriet had always hated the town. At eighteen years of age she, the daughter of the town's leading Orangeman, had fallen in love with a Roman Catholic from the Free State; had left it in a blaze of scandal. She had shaken the dust of it from her feet forever, she thought, but the tide of war had carried her back and left her beached in the old town. During her only visit back with her daughter - a fruitless trip to see her mother who was dying - a bomb had destroyed her home in London, killing both her husband and her young son.

Harriet was a woman who lived a lonely desperate life. In the evening, when her work was done, she would sit on a straight-backed kitchen chair and stare into the red coals that shifted and pulsed behind the bars of the black stove. Kate used to sit opposite and watch her face intently. She knew her mother could see something in the coals that she could not see.

Sometimes her eyes gleamed, sometimes they grew dark and apprehensive, then at other times an expression of exquisite happiness would cross her face. This would quickly fade to be replaced by a secret knowing smile.

But what frightened Kate most was when her mother gazed into the fire with an expression of such grief that Kate would grow sad watching her. Then she knew her mother inhabited a world of memories that she could not enter.

Then there were the days that she had seen *them*, her two Protestant sisters who lived at the other end of the town. They ignored her, of course, cut her dead and as she stared into the red depths of the fire she relived her humiliation over and over. She had never discussed her past with Kate, never explained how they happened to be Catholic, living in a Catholic ghetto, while her family was the wealthiest Protestant family in the town. Yet, she expected Kate to share her interest in them, her sense of devastation when either one of them was snubbed.

"Did you see one of *them*?" she would ask if Kate came home looking upset.

Kate would nod silently.

"Which one?"

"The gingery one."

Kate always referred to them as the gingery one and the dark one. It seemed too familiar to call them by name when she had never spoken to them.

"Did you see *him*?" she would ask when Kate came home from watching the Twelfth of July parade pass through the town on the way to Finaghy.

"Yes."

"Where was he? Out at the front? I suppose he was

in full dress?"

"He was wearing white gloves and a bowler hat.
And a big orange sash."

The ghost of a smile would cross her mother's face.

"They all wear white gloves and bowlers."

Harriet would sit staring into the fire, her mind
petrified in the past.

"He always loved a good breakfast the morning of
the Twelfth. Porridge, followed by bacon and eggs,
soda farls, potato bread. I was the one who cooked
him his breakfast. He wouldn't eat it unless I made it
for him."

"What happened?"

Kate would watch her for the next sentence which
would tell her how it all ended.

But it never came.

* * *

Kate stood beside her mother while she picked her
'rig out' for the closing of the Mission the following
Sunday: she saw Harriet humbly listening to the shop
assistant's advice, saw her thickening figure and
greying hair and a wave of feeling went through her.
Why did Harriet feel that she had to go to the Mission
every year? This woman didn't care about mass
contrition, competing for style, she had no interest in
sitting at the back of the church to watch and criticise
her neighbours. She was too individual for that. Kate
realised that her mother was trying desperately to
conform, be one of the townspeople and they were so
much less than she was.

"Thank goodness I got that, I must say it's a load off
my mind. The shops will be cleaned out by the end of

the week. You know what the style is like for the closing of the Mission," she said one year as she carried the bag with the new suit carefully down the stairs of the shop. "Do you think it would be noticed if I wore my green hat instead of getting a new one? And by the way Miss, you will have to come with me this year. You're sixteen now, it's expected of you."

"We have our own retreat at school, the nuns prefer us to do that." Kate could have added that the nuns were a middle-class order who seemed to disapprove of the evangelical nature of the annual Mission. "Besides we have to study for the 'O' levels. But Martha Grey asked me to go with her on Thursday night. I'll go then."

"Yes, I'll let you go with her then, but you're coming with me every other night," said Harriet who hated going alone.

* * *

The great Cathedral was packed.

Kate could not believe that there were so many women in the town - and these were only the Catholics. Latecomers were still pouring in, stewards patrolled the aisles reverently in rubbersoled shoes, whispering to people to move closer in their seats, finding it more and more difficult to find places for everybody. The middle aisle, where Kate sat beside her mother, had as always filled up first, nobody wanted to sit in the 'penny aisle' on the left which was so far away from the pulpit that everyone came out with a crooked neck, nor would they sit in the 'poor aisle' on the right. The people who sat there never had any new clothes even for the closing of the

Mission, they wore headscarves instead of hats, they did not sing the hymns out loud, they kept their heads bowed when they went to communion, they were humble.

The altar dominated the Cathedral, it loomed in front of Kate, a huge edifice in white marble. She knew that if she went close to it and stared into it that it would be threaded with small veins like the inside of an infant's arm and that if she leaned her hand on it, its touch would be cold on the hottest day, a coldness that would numb her palm and send jabbing pains along her arm. She ached to reach out and touch it, then to reach down to the ground and feel the texture of another kind of marble in the mosaic patterns of the floor. Her fingers itched to touch and feel the starched white of the altar cloths, the rich red pile of the carpet which ran up the steps of the main altar. She wanted to climb and stroke the wounded figure of the plaster Christ, nailed to a wooden cross which He carried forever from station to station around the walls of the church.

Harriet nudged her to pay attention and she straightened herself and folded her hands in her lap. How she longed to be like her mother who waited for the Missioners with a quiet grace. Kate looked at her and saw the gentle face rapt with concentration, her thoughts, unlike Kate's, were not a jumble of colours, words, textures. Young as she was, she recognised that Harriet's mind was not like her own.

Kate hated going to the Mission, hated the feelings of subservience she had towards the priests who ran it, hated to be among masses of women. It was always the same: three priests from one of the religious orders. Masters of showmanship. Each order had a different style of dress but all were startling in their dramatic effect. Some were stark in long black cassocks with huge crucifixes on their chests. Others wore heavy cream surplices with short capes and richly coloured cummerbunds, but they had a common way of capturing the attention of the worshippers. They never appeared in the pulpit until the Church was packed, and the congregation was growing restive, then they always arrived with a prop, a prayer-book or a small black biretta which, before a sea of interested eyes, they balanced delicately on the edge of the pulpit before they greeted the populace and then, with the tension in the church at breaking point, they bellowed out the first lines of the sermon.

The Mission always opened on a Monday night with a priest who spoke of the wrath of God with evangelical zest. Monday night was always known among the younger and more irreverent as 'Blood and Thunder' night. And afterwards, the women of the parish would hurry home to fulfil their wifely duties, thoughtful, subdued and not a little frightened.

On Tuesday night the joker arrived. He would lean companionably on the pulpit propped up on an elbow. "Did ye hear yer man last night? I bet ye were quaking in yer shoes. I'll tell ye this but don't let on to him. I was back there in the sacristy listening - and I was rattling too. Now we'll try to remember a few things he said. I heard him say that God is infinitely Just but I didn't hear him say that He is infinitely Merciful ..."

The third night was the aesthetic. He was usually refined in appearance, in speech. Here there were no threats, no cajoling, just a plain statement of the teachings of the Church, with a built-in warning for those who transgressed. Kate looked at the tired women seated around her. They had rushed all day to find the time to get out for an hour at night. Now they were sitting in the brightly lit church being harangued by a man in the pulpit.

"When I was in Rome for the Holy Year ... " he was saying.

She was certain that none of the women around her had been on holiday for years.

There was a priest sitting inside the altar waiting to say Benediction. Four altar boys in frilled white surplices yawned their way through the sermon as they sat on the steps of the altar. No female was allowed to go inside the altar rails or to sing in the choir whose members were now filing out to the Lady Chapel to sing the Benediction hymns ...

Beside her Harriet nudged her again.

"Pay attention, you're sitting with your mouth open, catching flies."

At last it was over.

The women poured out of the church, amazed that it was still bright outside. The air felt warm after the cold within.

"You're an awful wee fidget to sit beside in the chapel ... sprawled all over the seat ... do they teach you nothing about deportment at that school?"

"I can't help it, my mind wanders ... I can't sit and pray all the time the way you do."

"Pray?" Harriet gave one of her rare smiles. "I wasn't praying, I was watching the people coming in thinking that some women are neither shape nor make. With some of them a good Spirella corset wouldn't go amiss!" She frowned. "I kept thinking of a poem I learned at school, 'tall ones, small ones, fat ones, thin ones' ... I think it's about cats."

"Rats," Kate said. "It's a poem about rats."

They walked through the quiet town in the mellow evening light. Kate, wanting to extend the time that she spent with her mother away from the dark house, stopped at all the shop windows and gazed in.

"Mrs Grey couldn't go because she wasn't churched after having her baby. What does that mean?"

"We're told it's a blessing on the mother ... although it seems more like a purification ritual to me."

"I thought that having a baby was a holy thing."

Harriet looked uncomfortable.

"I don't agree with everything the Church does - some things seem almost pagan." Then, with a flash of anger, "Anyway I wish you'd give over with your silly questions, you've my head moidered."

* * *

On Thursday night Kate went to the mission with Martha. 'Blood and Thunder' had returned to give the women a talk on company keeping. The priest spoke of the dangers of courting, french kissing, passionate kissing and all the sins of the flesh that could be committed in lonely places after darkness fell. Kate listened fascinated, amazed at how much this strange priest knew of what went on in her town. It seemed to be a much more interesting place than she had ever known it to be.

"He seems to know a lot about us for a stranger," she whispered to Martha when he mentioned what had been seen going on in Millar's Hill after dark.

"Divine Inspiration," Martha whispered back.

Afterwards they walked back through the town. When they came to the corner where Martha turned down to go to her own house, she said to Kate,

"Why don't you walk around the green with me before you go home? There's great crack down there at night."

"What kind of crack?"

"You'll see."

They paraded along the path that bordered the green. Kate was tall and thin, Martha was short and wide. Suddenly Martha reached out and caught Kate by the arm and grasped it tightly. Kate walked along feeling selfconscious with Martha clinging to her stiffly held arm. Through the sleeve of her cardigan she could feel an embarrassing heat from Martha's soft, low breast, from her strong sinewy body she could smell the faint odour of woman. With a feeling of revulsion she attempted to withdraw her arm but wordlessly Martha tightened her hold - she was armlocked in a grip of pseudo-friendship. Three boys passed - walking as aimlessly as they were - in the opposite direction. They smirked towards the girls as they passed. When they had gone, Martha said.

"We'll turn here."

And under the shade of the overhanging trees they turned in the half light and walked slowly down the green again. A few boys and girls had gathered at the end of the green - some sat on railings, some stood on the grass in the shadows away from the street lights. There were about twenty of them altogether in a wide ragged circle, the shy ones remaining on the periphery, not wanting to be there but drawn to it by something they did not comprehend.

Martha and Kate leaned across the railings, staring into the dusky green.

The three boys walked past them again.

"Do you know those boys?"

"Yes, the tall dark one is Tony Kelly. He thinks all the girls are crazy about him. The boy with him is Paddy McGuinness. He's a nice guy."

"And the other one?"

"That's Benny Maguire - he's dying."

"Dying?" Kate turned around and looked at him.

"He has consumption, his lungs are riddled with it. He's a patient in the sanatorium, sometimes he gets home for a few days. He's not supposed to go out but the lads call for him and bring him for a wee walk."

The three boys had stopped and turned on the path above them and were coming down past them again. In the warm June night two of the boys were wearing open-necked shirts, carrying light sports jackets over one shoulder. Kate looked and saw the stooped figure in the heavy tweed overcoat walking close to the railings. Even as she watched she saw him stop and take a white handkerchief from his pocket. As his friends waited he bent forward and coughed into it.

"When he coughs like that he's coughing blood into his hanky, so Tony told me. It means he hasn't long to live. My mother says that he will go at the fall of the leaf," Martha said. "That's when they go with that complaint."

The fall of the leaf.

Kate stared towards the sick boy and suddenly he was imbued with romance. Great composers died of consumption, poets faded away with it, brilliant writers were cut down in their prime. She was sure they had all died at the fall of the leaf. Her heart beat faster as the boys approached on the path behind them and passed by again. They moved a little way below where the girls stood and for a few moments they leaned on the railings, then suddenly Tony Kelly vaulted the railings and moved onto the grass. His friend Paddy McGuinness leapt over after him. Together they held their fists in the air and danced around, goodhumouredly tipping at each other, parodying a boxing match. Then Tony caught his friend in a headlock and they rolled onto the ground. Martha moved from Kate's side.

"I'd better stop them. They'll kill each other."

On short muscular legs she walked towards them, leaned forward and began to pull Tony up by the arm. Laughing he reached up and pulled her down. The moment he touched her Martha fell and Tony knelt beside her, pinning her two arms above her head. Then he leaned over and kissed her. Paddy McGuinness stood up and walked away, dusting grass from his clothes and grinning sheepishly.

"Let me go, Tony Kelly," Martha shouted kicking her legs. "I can't move my arms."

Kate, looking at Martha's strong muscular arms and Tony's skinny ones, felt surprised. But further down the green figures were moving from the path and the railings onto the grass. She stood alone listening to the squeals and shrieks coming from the middle of the green. It was growing darker every moment but she could see the black outlines of coupled figures silhouetted against the brighter horizon.

She heard a cough and looking down she saw Benny Maguire leaning against the railing. He was looking towards her. Quickly she looked away but

not before she saw, with a terrible pity, the stark
outlines of his emaciated face.

That night she dreamed about him, he was in a
garret writing poetry, he had long hair and wrote
with a quill pen. He looked straight towards her and
she saw again the unearthly beauty of his doomed
eyes.

"Are you going to the Mission tonight?" she asked
Harriet the following day.

"I'll give it a miss tonight," her mother said, looking
guilty.

"Is it alright if I go out to confession?"

"There's no confession on a Friday."

"They're making an exception this week because of
the Mission."

How glibly she lied. How bland her face was, how
smooth her voice.

Fool! she wanted to shout to Harriet. Don't believe
me, don't trust me. Question me the way Martha's
mother questions her.

But Harriet only looked at her and said.

"Aye, that's alright but don't be late home."

The examinations had finished at last, the school
had closed for the Summer holidays so she wasn't
able to use the excuse of studying in somebody's
house for getting out in the evenings. As she walked
through the town in the dusky evening she told
herself that she was not going to the green, she was
going to Ciara's house. Ciara was her best friend, not
Martha. But Ciara was dull now and Kate knew that
they would go into her sittingroom and play scrabble.
Ciara's mother would make them lukewarm cocoa
and Kate would get up and leave at nine o'clock.

The green lured her.

When she came to the intersection she turned off in that direction.

Again there was a scattered crowd of young people hanging around the end of the green. Martha came over to her.

"Did you see the way that Tony Kelly was chasing after me last night? I nearly died when he pulled me down to the ground." She tossed her greasy brown hair back. "He's crazy about me."

"Here he comes," Kate said.

Tonight there were only two of them. Tony and Benny.

"Hello girls," Tony grinned sheepishly. Benny stood a little way behind, smiling shyly at them. Again he was wearing a heavy tweed overcoat with the collar turned up. In the evening light Kate could see the chiselled bones of his face. Even the faint yellow tones of his skin seemed attractive. He was looking towards her, and she saw something like longing in his eyes. At the fall of the leaf he would be dead. She turned and walked away, her heart too full for words. Martha followed her. The two boys trailed behind. They came to the top of the green where the path narrowed and led to a wilder part, a hilly place, full of trees and bushes. The path which led from one to the other was narrow and rutted. When they crossed over Kate turned around and saw that Benny was lagging behind - he looked deathly pale and as he came nearer she could hear his strained breathing. Letting the others walk ahead, she waited for him. She held her hand out and helped him over the rough ground, noticing his narrow white hands and thin wrists - a poet's hands. Ahead she saw Martha and Tony walk arm-in-arm then they turned off the main path into the trees. She felt Benny's arm slide around her waist. Shyly she moved closer to him.

"Do you write much poetry?" she asked him.

"Poetry?" he was looking at her in amazement. "What the hell would I be doing writing poetry."

It was the first time that she had ever heard him speak and his voice was deep and rough. There was a silence and she could hear him wheeze softly as he walked along. Suddenly and with surprising strength he caught her by the arm and pushed her off the path.

"Here, we'll go over to yonder bushes. I know you feel the way I do - mad for a coort."

* * *

Kate lay on the leather chair beside the fire, her eyes closed. She was deathly tired, had felt exhausted since she had gone back to school in September. When she had come in from school today her mother had told her that Benny Maguire had died up in the San. Now Harriet stood beside her holding the plate of dinner she had refused to eat.

"It's a lovely wee bit of sirloin," she was saying. "You've been so pernickety about your food lately that I went out and got it especially for you."

Kate was suddenly shaken with a fit of sobbing and coughing.

"What ails you daughter?" Harriet looked alarmed.

"It's Benny Maguire,"

"Benny Maguire?" said Harriet mystified. "His death is very sad, him being the only son of a widowed mother and only seventeen but you didn't know him ... it's not like you to show your feelings, you're usually as deep as a draw well."

But Kate, lying listless and withdrawn on the chair beside the old stove, didn't answer.

"It wouldn't do you any harm to go down and see the doctor tonight, Miss" Harriet said at last. "You look as though you need a good tonic."

Kate opened her eyes and looked at her mother.

"I'll go down if you come with me."

The doctor examined her carefully, weighed her, asked her if she had a cough. He was not Harriet's doctor - when the National Health Service was implemented she had gone to Dr McAdam who had been in the town since she was a child. To her surprise, Kate had insisted on giving her medical card to Dr Steele.

"But you don't know him."

"He's Ciara's doctor, I like him."

Now he turned around to Harriet.

"She's definitely anaemic, so I'm putting her on iron. I'm giving her a cough bottle." He turned to Kate, "I would like another look at you, that's a nasty cough ... come down a week from today."

They thanked him and got up to leave.

"I've lumps all over my legs," Kate said as they reached the door of the surgery. Harriet and Steele stared at her. "Big flat red ones," she said. "They're all over my shins."

"Sit down, Kate," the doctor said "And take your stockings down."

"This is the first I've heard of it," Harriet said, flushed and annoyed as they watched Kate peel her black school stockings over her knees. She rolled the heavy tops over her garters to cover them. Steele knelt down and examined her legs carefully.

"Pull your stocking up, child," he said at last, rising

to his feet and going over to wash his hands in the wash-hand basin. He sat down again at his desk and scribbled out a letter. He folded it and put it into an envelope and handed it to Harriet.

"Bring that out to the Chest Hospital tomorrow morning," he looked towards Kate. "The Sanatorium. I'm sending you for a chest x-ray. They'll have the results almost immediately and the specialist out there will have a chat with you." He sighed "I'll have his report the following morning ... I'll be in touch with you."

And that was all. Clumsy and mystified Kate and Harriet bumbled towards the door. There they crashed into each other and bumped their heads together. Steele watched them, unsmiling. Harriet rubbed her head and looked towards him.

"What about the prescriptions? Do we still bring them to the chemist?"

"The prescriptions, the chemist?" Like them he seemed to be in a daze.

"No, no give them back to me." He tore them across and dropped them into the waste paper basket.

"We're starting from scratch."

* * *

"I was so scared that day," he told Kate afterwards. "I should have known you had tuberculosis the minute I examined you. The cough was there, you had lost weight, you even mentioned night sweats - and I nearly let you walk out through the door."

It wasn't until she mentioned the lumps on her legs that he realised how ill she was. *Erythema Nodosum* they were called and their presence nearly always denoted a tubercular infection. He knew then that she would have to go to bed and stay there for a long time. Complete bed rest, he called it. But things were not all black. Her sputum test proved negative - which meant that her condition was not infectious so she was able to stay at home and attend the hospital as an out-patient, she only had to go for x-ray and to attend the specialist every two months. The disease had been caught in the early stages. It was an infection and very recent in origin. Dr Steele came up to the house and told Harriet that she too would have to have a chest x-ray. She could have caught the infection from Kate or indeed could have been infected and passed it on. Had they associated with anyone who was suffering from tuberculosis? If there was somebody going around with such a virulent strain of the disease the health authorities would want to know about it. Harriet wracked her brains and said that she didn't know anyone with TB. Of course she knew how serious it was, it was only a few days since a youngster in the town had died of the disease. Where, they pondered, could she have caught it? They looked towards Kate for inspiration. She thought she saw an accusing look in their eyes.

"There was a nun in school," she said, "Who used to cough blood into her handkerchief. We could see it. She used to lean over my desk and cough and cough. Then she went back to Dublin. Ciara's mother heard that she had consumption."

Harriet looked at Steele.

"Surely she couldn't have caught it like that?"

"There's a chance that she could, it's a droplet infection." He was so angry that Kate felt frightened. "I might have known. Those bloody nuns, they would still be out teaching children if they had foot and mouth disease."

Chapter Two

Kate sat at the window at the foot of the bed and waited for Steele.

Through the window she could see to the end of the street where the old stone houses on her side converged with the plaster-fronted ones opposite. The sky was clear and blue but the winds that whipped the trees around the Cathedral were icy cold. Cold, too, was the glint of sunlight on its ancient stone turret. Both cold wind and bright sunlight by-passed the narrow street. Pot-holes overflowed with last night's rain and rainbows of oil.

Across the street, Lizzie Trodden stood pedestalled on the stone steps of her hall. Her arms were folded to support forgotten breasts, her head pivoted and turned as her eyes recorded information. Her roving eye caught sight of Kate behind the lace curtain, the blinds, the drapes - barriers Harriet had erected between themselves and the outside world. Lizzie's head stopped turning, the eyes sought her out, found her, focussed on her.

She retreated from the window frightened, the watcher watched. She crawled stiffly down the bed and climbed between starched white sheets. She sat with the back of her neck pressed against the brass bedrail - deliberately uncomfortable. Her bed faced two narrow windows. The window to the right of her bed faced the old Protestant Cathedral, high behind the houses across. The one to the left looked out onto the Catholic Cathedral which stood on a more distant hill. In the valley between lay the town. A cloud shaped like a car appeared on the sky of the Catholic window.

"If that cloud is the same shape when it reaches the Protestant window, Steele will come today."

She slid down the bed and closed her eyes. The bed was icy cold, her feet were numb. It was two years earlier and she was cycling through country lanes. She pedalled furiously.

"Here, here, what's going on?"

Harriet stood at the bedroom door, carrying her breakfast tray.

"Oh," Kate sat up. "My feet are freezing."

"Aye, it's a wee bit cold alright. I must get you a hot water-bottle."

Kate lifted a small folding table from the side of the bed and put it in front of her.

"Did you know that it's very bad form to present a

tray without a tray cloth?"

"Yes," Kate said, looking at the elegant Irish lace tray cloth, covering a rusting tin tray.

Harriet walked to the window.

"Were you at them curtains?"

"No," Kate looked at her wide-eyed and innocent - but Harriet knew she was lying. She stepped back and compared them with the curtains on the other window.

"You were at them, look at them bunched and gathered on one side - it had to be you."

"It wasn't me."

Her voice rose in a wail of self-pity. Now she actually believed she had not bunched the curtains, that she was being blamed, in the wrong again.

"Sure I could see oul' Trodden gawking over. I knew she was looking at something."

Harriet continued to lecture and Kate whined and anxiety trod the air between them.

Kate had one of her imaginary conversations with her secret mother.

"Why doesn't Steele come?" she would ask

"Well, my dear, there must have been an emergency, some kind of an accident," Harriet would say. "Something has happened, otherwise he would be here by now."

"He was to bring me a letter, you know, the results of my x-ray."

"Yes dear, but you know that it will be good news and that your lungs will be perfect."

"The specialist said I had put on weight and I looked very well."

"We know that, dear girl, and he was right. You do look well and you'll get word today that you can get up."

"And go out?"

"Of course."

"I've been here for nearly two years, looking out through these windows and I can't take much more of it. I'm afraid at night, there seems to be something out there in the old graveyard, nothing I can see. A presence."

"Yes dear, I know what you mean."

"And *Dizzy Sense* is on the wall."

"Nightmares, dear, we all have them."

*   *   *

Harriet craned her neck as she pleated the curtains.

"There's a car. It's the doctor and he's stopping outside the door. Here give me that tray and I'll bring it down with me, I don't want to keep him waiting outside and give oul' Trodden something to gawk at ..."

Kate had forgotten the cloud.

Now she looked through the Protestant window. It was passing over - disintegrating, it had fanned out and looked like a bus. She heard Steele's impatient rattle at the letterbox and her mother's step as she went to open the front door. She heard a greeting of mock surprise and the door closed. They stayed in the hall, it was directly under her bedroom, she could hear the drone of their voices.

They were talking about her.

She hung out of the bed from the waist and put her ear to the ground where gnarled floorboards joined under cheap linoleum. She could hear nothing.

"It's bad news," she thought, "I'm dying."

She lay back on the pillow and closed her eyes. She could feel her strength ebb away, a weakness stole over her, holding her arms to the bed with invisible weights.

"Tuberculosis," she could hear people say. "She just faded away."

"Well darling, having a nap?"

She opened her eyes and saw Steele standing over her bed. He brought an aura of fresh cold air to the sick-room. He put his bag on the ground and then walked over to the window where he stood with his back to Kate, looking out.

"You've a great view of the Cathedral from here."

As he spoke he took a letter from the inside pocket of his coat and stared at it for a moment. Then he came over and sat at the bottom of the bed.

"Were you expecting me sooner?"

"Yes, but it doesn't matter ..."

"I had an early morning call, I've just got back to collect the post. Look Kate, there's no easy way of saying this to you - I think you should read this letter yourself."

Kate held it with shaking hands. For a moment the writing was a blur, then the bottom line cleared and jumped at her.

"In the meantime the patient will continue to have complete rest. We will review her case in three months time ..."

Steele was watching her. His back was turned to the window and she could not see his eyes but she could feel a deep sympathy flowing towards her.

"Start at the beginning, not the end."

"What difference does it make, I'm not getting any better."

"Here, give it to me."

He folded it and put it back in his pocket. Kate began to cry. He took a handkerchief from his pocket leaned over and clumsily dabbed her eyes.

"I know you're disappointed, so am I. It's coming up to two years now." He was looking around him. "God, but this is an awful big barn of a room, a body could get awful lonely up here."

"I get frightened, I think I'm going to die."

She thought he might laugh but he just stared at her for a moment then said.

"What put that into your head?"

"Benny Maguire had tuberculosis and he died."

"So that's it. Give me your hands, I want to say something to you."

Shyly she reached her hands towards him, he took them in his and she felt the warmth and the strength emanating from him. I would trust this man forever, she thought, and as though she had spoken aloud he said,

"You trust me, don't you Kate? I want to tell you something, look at me and you'll know that I'm telling the truth. Benny Maguire had two cavities in his lungs the size of oranges. The poor wee bugger hadn't a chance, he was too far gone when we got him."

Poor Benny. She was silent, remembering. She looked up at Steele and he was watching her ...

"You knew Benny, didn't you?"

She nodded.

"I thought so, there was an expression on your face, you wouldn't have looked so sad about somebody you'd never met. Now," he continued, "you have a small lesion on your left lung which has calcified."

"Well, then ..."

"You should have read all of the letter ... you would have seen that your blood sedimentation rate is sky high and that means there are toxins in your bloodstream - so we can't let you up." He dropped her hands and stood up, walked to the Catholic window and stared blindly through it. "A high BSR means that there's still infection in your body. The worrying thing is that it should have cleared long before now."

He came over and sat on the end of the bed again.

"Your appetite is good?"

"Yes."

"Sleep ... No problem there?"

She shivered.

"I don't sleep very well."

"Why not?"

"I suppose I doze too much during the day."

She looked to the corner of the room. The ceiling was white, innocently bare. The flocked wallpaper bulged, swollen by a patch of damp plaster. But she had gone, that obscene mouthing creature who would be there tonight. Steele followed the direction of her gaze and looked puzzled. He reached for his bag and stood up.

"Well," he said, smiling down at her. "I'm off to enjoy myself, today's my halfday."

"Are you going to the pictures?"

That's what she would do if she had an afternoon to herself.

He laughed.

"No, no, I'm not interested in films, I take myself off

to the country." He narrowed his eyes still looking at her. Then he said.

"Maybe you would like to come with me?"

She wondered if he was joking and watched him carefully to judge the tone of his next remark.

"Would you like to come with me? If I could keep you awake for the afternoon you might sleep tonight."

Her heart gave a great leap when she realised he wasn't teasing her. Now he grinned and suddenly he looked young and boyish.

"Yes, you must come. Doctor's orders - you can sit in the car and look around you. I won't keep you out too long."

At the bedroom door he stood with his hand on the handle.

"You haven't answered, but I think we have a date. I'll call for you at two."

When she heard the click of the front door and knew that Steele had gone she slipped out of bed. She did everything by stealth. She could open the heavy door of the bedroom without making a sound, she knew how to stop pulling it an instant before it creaked, then slide it gently open. She could walk along the old varnished floorboards of the landing without making a sound, her feet suctioned to the polished linoleum strip which ran down the centre. Downstairs, through the mahogany bannisters, she could see the glow from the old black stove. The red stone floor shone with it. Her mother sat at a table by the window and drew circles on the white damask tablecloth with the back of a monk's spoon. Kate could see her stiffen and listen but Harriet could not be sure that she was out of bed. She knew where the squeaky boards were, how to set foot lightly on them and gradually increase her weight. She always felt like an unwanted visitor in somebody else's house. Even when Harriet went out shopping she went through the house by stealth.

"Can I come down?"

Harriet stiffened with surprise, then craned her neck to where her daughter watched her through the bannisters. She stood up.

"Get back into bed, you're not allowed down."

"For a minute, please."

"No, I'll be up now, I'll bring you a cup of tea."

She padded back to bed and sat up. She would be out for an hour or two this afternoon but after that she would be here for another three months with her two windows. Panic gripped her throat, a clammy sweat covered her body. How could she live through it, live another three months, another bad report, another ... She clenched her knuckles and sank her teeth into them. The pain distracted her mind, relieved the tension. She could hear her mother's footstep on the thin lino of the stairs. She came into the room carrying the tea carefully.

"I'm not allowed to get up."

"Aye, the doctor explained. But it's just a wee setback, it's for your own good. I'm sure they know best. What's that on your hand?"

She craned forward.

"What? Nothing, I just slept on it."

She put her cup down and slid her hand under the bedclothes.

"The doctor says he'll bring me out to the country this afternoon."

Harriet turned and gave her daughter a smile of

extraordinary sweetness untouched by envy. At times like this, Kate was stunned by her mother's beauty and mourned for her locked in this prison, made partly by circumstances and partly by her own mind.

"He thinks that a change of scenery might do you good, I know that he'll look after you, see that you don't get too tired. It's very good of him to take the trouble. Most doctors couldn't care less, these days."

"He's very good for a Protestant."

"Indeed he is," Harriet said. "You get that oul' Murphy crawthumping at the altar every Sunday and I mind the time when he wouldn't cross the door to visit a sick child unless he was paid in advance. That was before the Health Scheme. Now the Catholics are all running to him with their Medical Cards. I'm sure that Dr Steele feels bitter. Half of them never paid him for calls in those days, now the same gang are running to thone oul' rip because he's a Catholic."

She went over and began to pleat the curtain again.

"Maybe Mrs Steele will come," Kate said. "He'll probably bring his children."

The hand that pleated the curtain stopped.

"Dr Steele has no children ... his wife is in a delicate condition."

Kate plucked the white cover on the bed.

"I see."

* * *

What was she going to wear?

~~he~~ had been tempted to ask her mother but she
~~   ~~ she would tell her to wear her school uniform
~~   ~~ had done for her x-rays. No, if she was going
~~   ~~ e afternoon with Steele she was not wearing

a gym-slip - she would dress for the occasion. She crept to the wardrobe in the corner of her room. Her black serge skirt hung neatly in the cupboard, and very little else. Behind the blazer and the burberry coat hung a grey gor-ray skirt with a single pleat at the front. It was her first adult skirt, bought the Christmas before last. She had only worn it a few times. She laid it on the bed and searched through the bottom drawer of the wardrobe. There she found a red shetland jumper with a polo neck. She pulled the clothes on quickly and trembling with excitement looked in the mirror. She recoiled in horror. She had always lived happily in her small straight body, she swam in the quarry with the local boys, climbed trees, played rounders. Puberty stroked and left her. The illness which attacked her lungs left her thin and pale. She had outgrown her strength, they said when they looked at her, nodded wisely to her mother and said that she would fill out later, that it was all going into her height.

Now she looked at herself in the mirror. No exercise and a high fat diet had changed her shape completely. Now she had a woman's body, definite breasts, a round tummy, buttocks and thighs. Words like 'fleshy' and 'bosomy' swam around in her head. Nausea gripped her throat. She stared at the white child's face atop the heavy body and the frightened face stared back at her. A scene from her childhood came into her mind - of a wake in a country farmhouse she had gone to with Ciara and Ciara's mother. They had stayed the night. Kate had been put to bed early, tucked to the inside of a double bed while the family and friends stayed up all night to wake the corpse. They slept in relays. Before dawn, when the first heavy sleep was over she was wakened by a soft hissing noise, the sound of women whispering as they undressed in the early hours.

The hissing became a mumble as teeth plunged into cups of water. Large buttocks were eased out of pink laced corsets and discreetly scratched. Massive brassieres were hung over brass bedends where they glowed with satin luminosity in the early light. She was lifted to the middle of the bed and soft fleshy bodies encompassed her's. The springs on the bed beside her's creaked with vain protest as heavy bodies were lowered into it. Then they began to talk. Not the women's talk she had always been used to, of how to set jam and starch pillowcases but a different talk for which they used different tones. Voices full of suggestion and the unsaid. They talked of childbirth and breastfeeding, of periods and young pregnant girls. They knew about mastoids and clots and how to cut a cord.

And a sweet sweaty smell of women filled her lungs.

Is this what she would become?

Had she no choice?

Her mother had never become one of these women, never discussed the human body, never touched Kate as far as she could remember, recoiled when she had ever touched her. But she lived apart from other women and they hated her. And so Kate had lived content in her neuter's body, had never thought that it would be any different. Already the grey skirt was creasing where it strained across her hips.

She needed a corset.

Oh God no, please no.

But she needed something to cover her legs. After a

search in the drawer of her dressing-table she found two pairs of black school stockings and a pair of ankle socks rolled in a corner. She pushed them back into the drawer then carefully opened the door of her bedroom and padded across the landing. She had heard the click of the front door closing behind her mother as she left to go across the road to the little shop. Harriet did not like Kate going into her room and if she were downstairs she listened at the bottom of the staircase, asked her what she was doing in there and called her out. The room was, as always, in semi-darkness, the curtains halfdrawn. The furniture was solid mahogany, a bastard assortment of awkwardly shaped pieces that her mother had picked up at auctions when they came to the town. The patterned linoleum was highly polished. Kate slid the dressing-table drawer open and trawled through undergarments, knowing that Harriet always kept three pairs of stockings here: a new pair of nylons in an unopened cellophane bag, a pair of silk stockings washed and ready for Sunday and a pair of heavier mended stockings that she would wear tomorrow when she had washed the ones she was wearing today. She did not dare take the new nylons and she scorned the heavy lisle ones so nervously she took the silk stockings. She could hear her mother pull the string in the letterbox as she came back from the shops. She put the stockings on in her room, stood up and the heavy tops rolled around her knees. She hunted through her drawer again and found garters still attached to her school stockings since the day she had gone for the x-ray. She put them on and found them tight around her heavy thighs. Her shoes were flat brown with punched toe-caps, bought for school two years ago. Her coat when she put it on was short and tight so she left it open and saw that at least a foot of her skirt hung below it.

She sat at the window and waited for Steele.

Across the street she saw Minnie Corr turn the key in her shop door as she opened for the afternoon. She knew that the key was big and iron and old like the keys of all the doors along the street. Iron too was the strip that hooked into each side of the window and kept the green shutters in place. Now she was carrying the heavy wooden shutters into the shop, hobbling slowly and painfully on arthritic legs.

"Poor thing," Kate had said to her mother once as she watched her from the window.

"Poor thing, my hat," Harriet said, watching her with contempt. "She doesn't have to do that, the Corrs have plenty of money, they're loaded."

"But where would they get it?" Kate asked enviously. She didn't want anyone to be loaded when they themselves had no money.

"Them'uns always had money," her mother said with finality. "Even in my grandfather's day."

Shirley Cummins, her young assistant, swept the passage selfconsciously.

"Wasn't thone a desperate shower last night?"

Below the bedroom window Kate could hear her mother scrub a halfmoon of cleanliness around their front door. Minnie and Shirley continued their loud conversation and looked towards her hopefully. Their remarks were general and they were near enough for her to join in but she scrubbed diligently and did not raise her head.

"Backstreet habits," she would say later. "I was not brought up to shout across the street like that."

She worked like a demon scrubbing the stone window-sill, rubbing the old sash window until it squeaked with cleanliness and the letterbox rattled in protest as it was rubbed with Brasso. Upstairs Kate, still wearing her heavy outdoor coat, was growing tired and she lay back on her bed with her head on the pillow and listened. She thought of all the cloths in the big box her mother kept in the cupboard under the stairs, the cloth to put the Cardinal Red polish on the hall and kitchen and the cloths to polish it off, the black Brasso cloths and the soft polishing cloths. The window cloths and the black lead cloths for the stove. When she was asked to help her mother she mixed them up. She took all the soft polishing clothes and covered them with black lead, Cardinal Red and Mansion polish.

"Look, just leave it to me," Harriet would say in despair.

"Why?"

"Why? Because you're a wee clart, that's why. God help the man that gets you."

Which would leave Kate to go back to her books with a clear conscience.

*   *   *

She could hear the whine of Petie Nixon's bread van as he came down the road and parked outside the shop. He slammed the door of the van and whistled as he went around and opened the back door with a clatter. She stood up and moved to the window where she could see him, bending into the back of the van to pull out the trays of baps, soda farls and Paris buns forward, now walking into the shop pointing

69

his black patent shoes like a ballet dancer and carrying his tray of bread shoulder-high. His black hair was parted in the centre and his skin was smooth and olive. He had gentle brown eyes and a handsome clipped moustache; even the fawn baker's coat which flapped around his long legs could not detract from Petie's beauty.

He danced divinely - or so they said.

When she was younger Kate had loved the dance nights in King Street. They were held at weekends in the hall at the rear of an old Georgian house down the street from where she lived. Kate used to stand on the steps of the dancehall and watch the dancers go inside. They came in their dozens, the girls from Woolworths, from the ice-cream shops and the factories. Strong capable girls who worked hard by day, packing, sewing, cleaning, became magical creatures by night. They were curved and slim, tripping daintily along in their gold shoes and rustling skirts. Kate used to stand on the steps, close to the door, drowned in the smell of their perfume and their powder.

She wanted to get close to them, touch them, be one of them with shining hair and long slim legs.

British soldiers used to come dressed in rough khaki uniforms and black laced boots. Kate would stand alone outside the dancehall full of longing, until it was dark and the other children had long gone home and her mother would come to the door to look for her. She would stand close behind the pillars of the old Georgian doorway while Harriet craned her head up and down the street.

"Are you there, Kate?" she would say in her quiet voice. "It's time to come in."

And Kate would stand so still and quiet, not even breathing, that even the people passing into the dancehall would hardly know she was there. Then Petie would come down the street with his girlfriend. He always came late because she taught Commerce in the Technical school and he had to wait until the nightclasses were finished. At the door of the dancehall he would stop when he saw Kate.

"Who is this beautiful young lady?"

He would cast around for an answer.

"And what is she doing in a place like this?"

And Kate would smile with delight and forget that she was uncovering her big teeth as her hand pulled her skirt down nervously to cover her lumpy legs. Petie's girl was a Protestant and was madly in love with him. It was said she would probably 'turn' which made her acceptable in their midst. She had already been asked to leave her home and was living in a flat in the Catholic part of the town. This was another mark in her favour.

Only Harriet could not see it in its proper light.

"Silly fool, she'll regret it," she would say as she watched them from behind the lace curtain in the sittingroom. "Letting herself down for an eejit like that."

"She'll have Petie's people," Kate would say.

"It's not the same," Harriet's mouth would twist bitterly. "You can't break the rules and expect to get away with it. You can't renege on your own like that. She'll be neither fish nor fowl for the rest of her life."

On sultry summer nights the beat of Latin-American music throbbed over the back streets. Kate would lie awake in bed, her soul filled with a nameless yearning. In the airless back room she could hear the bedsprings creak as Harriet twisted and turned.

Some day I'll grow up and leave her in her lonely bed, she would think, I will go into that forbidden hall and dance the rumba with the soldiers. And then she would see herself, her legs magically long and slim, gyrating in the centre of a shiny floor with a blond loose-limbed soldier.

At last she saw Steele's car come into view, tilting on expensive springs, sliding silently to her front door. She heard the car door slam and then the rattle of the brass letterbox. The door opened and she heard him pounding up the stairs, her heart began to thump loudly and sweat poured down her back.

"Are you ready, child?"

She swayed with a sudden dizziness. He put an arm around her to support her and laughed.

"You're not used to being vertical."

Harriet stood at the bottom of the stairs and watched their slow descent.

"Goodbye," Steele said pushing Kate before him into the hall.

"Goodbye," Kate grinned selfconsciously, her hand already turning the brass knob of the hall door.

"Goodbye," said Harriet, retreating into the dark room.

* * *

She walked slowly, haltingly, along the crooked footpath. Steele opened the door of the car and helped her in, shut it firmly and walked around to the driver's seat. The car was full of sun, heat and the smell of new leather - it was merry with music.

Shirley Cummins sat on an upturned box in her shop window and craned her neck while old Mr Lavery halted his slow progress along the street, leaned heavily on his stick with both hands and peered into the car with bushy eyebrows. Up and down the narrow street lace curtains twitched and shivered. Steele turned and gave her a wide friendly smile, started the engine and they were off.

The big car came to the end of the street, stopped and turned down Dean's Hill which led to the border road: they were still in the poorer part of the Catholic quarter of the town. The people who lived here were descended from the mill people her mother had often told her about, they were clannish, inbred, suspicious. They peered from their doorways and halted on the broken pavements to watch Steele's progress down the hill. He drove slowly, careful of the children playing on the road. Almost all of them smiled and waved at him. Traitors, Kate thought, remembering what her mother had told her about them sneaking to Murphy with their medical cards. Suddenly he braked in the middle of the road and she was flung forward.

"Sorry pet," He put an arm out to save her. "I'm sure I saw that wee brat Tommy Mooney coming out of his front door. He knows he's confined to bed for the rest of the week."

"The Mooney's live there," Kate said ashamed that she knew such humble people but unable to deny them. He started the engine again and coasted slowly down the hill. In front she could see the thin outline of Tommy Mooney, head bent, walking quickly towards the bookmaker's shop at the corner.

Run Tommy, she shouted inwardly. He's after you.

Tommy turned and caught sight of Steele's car. His yellow face turned a shade paler, then he bent his head and dived through the groups of men who jammed the doorway of the bookie's shop. The racing season had started and the men of the town with time on their hands gathered here to listen to the racing results, blocking the hall and packing the greasy step. The ground in front of them was littered with cigarette butts. They parted to let Tommy through and closed ranks behind him, then stood in a solid mass watching Steele with puzzled grins as he pulled up outside.

"I don't know what they're leering at me for, I'd nearly go in there and drag that wee bastard out by the scruff of the neck."

He sat there drumming his fingers on the steering wheel, choking with anger.

"I'll have that wee bugger in hospital by Monday."

Kate looked at him covertly. His face was red and blotched with rage. She slid down in the seat of the car her heart thumping with fear. Steele's unpredictable behaviour was a legend in the town. It was rumoured that once when he had disagreed with a patient he had opened the front door of the surgery and thrown him bodily onto the street. He would lump all Catholics as being feckless and careless about their health. Any second now he might open the door of the car and order her out. She closed her eyes and waited. He gave a deep sigh and then started the engine again. Nervously, she stole a look at him. He seemed to have forgotten the incident. He was completely relaxed, all his concentration was on his driving. Gradually she too began to relax, she was no longer covered in a clammy sweat, her hands unclenched and her headache eased. She began to look around her. She had walked and cycled every road surrounding the town but now the scenery was changing, becoming unfamiliar. After several miles the car slowed down and he steered it into a grass verge beside a narrow bridge. He braked then turned to her and smiled.

"Now girl, out you get."

She clambered ungracefully out of the car, walked over to the bridge and leaned against it. The stone of the bridge was rough and hot. Underneath she could feel a deep coldness. She raked her fingers along the smooth green moss. A soft breeze fanned her face and ruffled her hair. She had sat at her window for almost two years and watched the world through glass. The sun, the wind and the rain were things that she could see but not feel. The church and the graveyard were static and unmoving. Now she felt the wind on her face and saw the river flowing. It tumbled along and the sound almost frightened her: she covered her ears. On either side of the river was the appleblossom, careless acres of pink and white spreading across the landscape.

Everything moved.

Clouds skudded across the sky, treetops swayed, the blossom shivered like delicate china. Kate forgot about Steele, her awe and fear of him. She breathed slowly, trying to imbibe the beauty of the scene before her - knowing even now that the image would stay with her forever.

He moved closer, pleased with her happiness.

"I knew you'd like it. I've been passing here for years and no matter how busy I am, I have to stop when the appleblossom is in bloom."

"I used to cycle out of the town to see it, but I have never seen ..."

She waved her hand.

"I know, it's here and it's gone - you have to catch it at the right time. Today is perfect."

She leaned her elbows on the bridge and pillowed her head on them.

"Are you tired?"

"Not in the least."

She was exhilarated.

"I want to show you something else."

He led the way down the side of the bridge and held his hand to help her down. She climbed slowly, treading gingerly over roots of trees, leaning heavily on his hand.

"Mind the muddy bits."

"I don't mind," she said, feeling nothing but pleasure as the wet earth squelched beneath her feet.

They were down, level with the river which roared past.

"Now look."

Along the edges of a dirt path under the trees and deep in the black earth, primroses lay in clumps, protected by delicate green ferns. They stretched as far as the eye could see. They must have bloomed here for generations, she thought, and nobody has ever seen but lovers. She smelled the wet earth, new leaves and the river. He walked over, picked a single flower and handed it to her.

"*Prima Rosa*," he said. "The first rose of Spring."

She held the delicate flower in her hand.

"How did you find it, this place?"

"I go fishing along here, this path goes on for miles. Further on you would see a carpet of anemones, I often watch them opening their petals to the sunlight and closing them again when a cloud comes to shut out the light. Some day I'll bring you right along it but you're not well enough yet."

He ambled off, peering at the ground and left her alone. It was a warm almost humid day and under the laced trees the trapped air was heavy with perfume. She drew the clean sweet air into her lungs, sweeping away the smell of blankets and her own sick body. She looked over at Steele who was now leaning against a tree trunk, his eyes narrowed, watching a hawk hovering over a clearing in the trees.

She walked over to him and timidly touched his sleeve.

"Thank you."

He straightened up in surprise, a middle-aged man in a heavy tweed sports-coat. He looked embarrassed, almost shy.

"We'd better be getting back."

He went ahead of her, leading them along the path towards the road. He was quick and nimble on his feet but slowed his pace deliberately so that she could keep up with him. From behind she could see that his dark hair was thinning at the crown. He had combed it carefully and covered it well but the merciless sun exposed a pink scalp under a single layer of hair.

"He's quite old," she thought and felt a pang of sympathy for him and for the little disguise which showed that he too was vulnerable. He turned around and held his hand towards her.

"Come on."

His hand was strong and warm. He pulled her up the final steep embankment onto the road.

"What a weight. It's like pulling a bullock out of a ditch."

He laughed and stood in front of her.

"Oh Kate, don't look so hurt, it's only a joke. You could do with losing a few pounds though, here." For a moment he was standing very close to her, his hands resting lightly on her hips. Then he walked around behind her and gave her a smart thump between the shoulder blades. "And straighten yourself up a bit."

He kept his arm around her shoulder as they walked towards his car.

"I'd love to stay out here all day, there are so many things I'd like to show you. But I have work to do and you have to be back in bed."

He opened the door of the car and she sat in. She would have to say something, talk to him. She racked her brains and then turned towards him with a bright smile.

"It must be wonderful being a doctor and helping people."

He looked at her and laughed.

"A man with a boil on his bum, there's nothing wonderful about that - nor about a lonely old woman aching to talk, just to talk, to hear the sound of her own voice ... Most of the work is routine, like any other job."

"But it must have its moments."

He thought.

"Yes, when a child is born, that's always wonderful ... Now we'll go for a short spin around the countryside, then I'll bring you home."

Steele continued to talk and Kate listened while she watched the sun shine through the dappled leaves of the wayside trees. No adult had ever chatted to her like this. In the strict discipline of the Convent where she went to school, the pupils were not encouraged to speak except when necessary. When they met Reverend Mother on the corridor they had to step aside and curtsey as she walked past. Silence was a virtue. At the tinkle of a handbell taken from a nun's wide sleeve, the pupils, boarders and daygirls, moved in long files, under supervision they ate their lunch in the school refectory, were watched while they changed for games - shivering as they stood at their lockers in long draughty corridors.

At home, the problems which her mother nursed as she sat by the fire at night were hers and hers alone.

* * *

How narrow the street was.

Two cars could barely pass each other. She sat in the front seat of Steele's car and saw it through a stranger's eyes. She had always hoped that it looked old and quaint, she knew now that it looked mean and miserable.

"We didn't always live here," she wanted to say. "Once we had a house in England with a long long garden."

He stopped the car in front of the house.

"Well, did you enjoy the spin?"

He switched the engine off, leaned back and smiled towards her. He was completely relaxed. Once again she was sweating, fists clenched, her jaw rigid. How could she thank him, she wondered, how could she get herself out of the car and over to the front door? The smallest social gestures were a nightmare to her.

As though he guessed, Steele leaned over and opened the door of the car: he started the engine as she got out and bumped her head on the door frame.

"Off you go and don't forget, straight to bed."

"Goodbye doctor."

She looked to the window above the front door almost expecting to see her own white face looking back. She pulled the string in the brass letterbox and opened the door. As she went through the hall she smelled the new polish, the door-handle freshly Brassoed. She stepped into the large gloomy room which at first she thought was empty until she saw her mother sitting at a table by the window with the *Irish News* spread on the table in front of her. She was engrossed in the crossword.

"Why are you sitting in the dark?"

Harriet started.

"I didn't hear you come in."

From where Kate stood she could see through the window the tips of the forest pines and the green sward of the distant golf-course.

From where Harriet sat she could see the grey wall which bounded the backyard.

"Was it a nice day?"

"Beautiful, did you not go out?"

"Well, there was no need. I did the shopping this morning."

Kate stood in the dark room and felt a wave of depression sweep over her. Her body felt young and it yearned for the sun, the wind, the flowers of today; she felt an urge to turn and run. She had to root her feet to the floor. Harriet stood up slowly.

"Give the fire a poke there and I'll make a wee cup of tea."

Kate lay back in the old leather armchair, smelled the fresh coal from the stove and the drawing tea from the kitchen.

"How old is Steele?"

Harriet came in carrying the teapot and put it on the side of the range. Her lips mumbled and counted.

"Wait 'til I see now, he'd be younger than me, but not that much. He'd be about thirty-eight, I suppose."

"He's quite old."

"He's quite young."

They spoke together and laughed.

"Did you go to school with him?"

"No, he came from outside the town somewhere, I think he went to boarding school. I knew him to see though. During the Summer holidays he used to come into town on a Saturday night to go to the dance in the town hall. He used to get off the bus outside our front door and I'd see him from the window. Even then he was handsome."

Kate looked at her in surprise.

"Steele handsome?"

"Oh yes, he was always considered very good-looking. Even then women chased him."

Harriet stared into the fire and a secret smile played around her lips. They ate the sandwiches. The kettle hissed and boiled. Harriet drew it to the side of the range away from the heat. Suddenly Kate was very tired, she could feel her legs trembling. But she wanted to stay there forever, safe with her mother, and never to go up to that room again. But Harriet was looking at the clock on the mantelpiece.

"Look at the time. Off you go to bed."

"I'd like more tea."

Harriet's voice rose.

"I said go."

She climbed the stairs reluctantly and walked along the newly-waxed landing. The air was warm from the sunny landing window and the heat from the kitchen range. She leaned down and looked through the mahogany bannisters to the room below. Her mother sat on a hardbacked chair and stared into the fire. Her hair was a dull black and her skin was smooth and creamy. High on the mantelpiece above her head the hands of the clock pointed to seven.

When she opened the door of her bedroom a blast of cold air hit her in the face. The room was always icy cold - even in Summer it had a deathly chill which seemed to permeate it from the graveyard across. Both windows were open at the top and the lace curtains writhed with an unseen force. The lino was shining and the clean pillow cases were pointed with stiff starched ears. She undressed slowly and tidied her clothes away, then climbed between white sheets and put her white hands on the white counterpane. Her books were piled on the floor beside her bed. She leaned over and lifted them up. Most of them were poetry books that she had collected since childhood, some of them were old school books. Usually, she pored over them murmuring the poems ... but tonight she looked at them without interest. She slid down the bed and heard them clatter onto the floor, closed her eyes and tried to sleep but she kept thinking of the books lying with twisted spines and crumpled pages. She leaned over and picked up a book at random. *The Oxford Book of English Verse*. I'll open it anywhere, read the first line and see if it applies to me. She tipped the book open and stared at the line at the top of the page.

"I'm half sick of shadows" said the Lady of Shalott.

She heard the book thump to the floor again as she turned, punched the stiff pillows and arranged them behind her head. Normally at this hour her bed was warm and untidy, she would get out to remake it and settle down contentedly enough to read for the night. Tonight was different. The river, the sun, the flowers made her pulses quicken, the sap that rose each Spring to green the bare trees around the old churchyard created a restlessness in her. She was quivering with longing, yearning to get out of this alien starched bed and live again. She crawled down the bed and sat on her hunkers at the window. The wee shop was closed, the street empty. Two figures appeared from around the corner of the street. Mary D'Arcy and Nellie going to the pictures, she thought. They waddled past twice a week, never missing a change of programme in the cinema. They were soon followed by more of the townspeople walking purposefully. Girlfriends, boyfriends, husbands, wives, sons and daughters, she knew them all. She listened to their conversation coming towards her and fading into the distance. When they laughed, she laughed, but was envious of them and their freedom, longed to be one of them. At last they had all passed by, the film began at half past seven. She moved swiftly to crawl up the bed and stopped as she heard a lone footstep in the distance, an exaggerated clop as the walker came down the echoing path which led from the old cathedral. She leaned forward to see who was coming. She could feel her head go light and whirl around. She clung to the bedrail for support, seeing her hands gripped whitely on the brass knobs that beaded the black enamel bed.

Billings.

He drew nearer, walking as always alone and close to the wall. Even from where she was she could see that his face had a prison pallor, his eyes staring from a skeletal face. Ten years in jail, that's what they said and now after seven or eight years he was creeping through the town again. Kate watched him with revulsion, peering after him until he was out of sight. She crawled along her bed and climbed in. She crouched down shivering and closed her eyes.

She never wanted to leave this bed, this room, again.

* * *

All of the children and none of the adults in the town knew that Billings was mad and strange and that he followed young girls. Sometimes he would stand at the side of the wall in King Street and watch the children play hopscotch on the footpath, or he would blend himself chameleon-like into the background of derelict houses and disused gateways that surrounded their play area. In the middle of a game they would suddenly feel uncomfortable, sensing that they were being watched, and turning around they would see him lurking in a doorway, an unpleasant man with his glittering eyes and the flush of excitement on his sallow cheek. An uneasiness would spread among them.

"It's Billings," somebody would say. "He's a bad egg."

And they would drift away from their game, older

ones shepherding younger ones away from a danger they could sense but not understand. Rumours abounded about him, searing their way through the network of children in the town and burning themselves out for lack of concrete evidence. Betty Quinn said he had followed her young sister home from her dancing class late one evening, padding behind her and disappearing into doorways when people came along. Gráinne Molloy said that he had sent her a note to meet him outside the old air raid shelter at eight one night but Kate did not believe her. Even then she sensed that Billings did not move in that way.

He lurked around and pounced on easy prey.

He did not frighten Kate. She saw him as an unpleasant character, ugly in the extreme with his gaunt face and his tombstone teeth, but she accepted him as part of the warp and the weft of the tapestry that formed her town. She felt secure and protected beyond the range of whatever havoc he desired to wreak among children. He did not pay any particular attention to her and she might never have had any contact with him if it had she not literally fallen into his lair. One day during the Easter break from school, she was coming from the shops, climbing the steep hill to her home and as usual she stopped at the top to draw her breath before she turned into King Street. Frankie Devlin came into view and pedalled frantically past her on an ancient bicycle.

"Get off the street, Kate" he yelled. "There's a mad bull down thonder escaped from the market."

Kate had just left the main street where the cattle market was held on the first Tuesday of every month. She had spent the last hour carefully sidestepping skidding cattle, hiding in shop doors as they lowed their way past, slithering and sliding on dung-filled streets. She had thought she was safe when she reached the quietness of King Street. Now, down the street she saw the bull. It was standing in the middle of the road just below her front door, surrounded by three drovers who were closing in on it. They shouted rough-voiced, brandishing pronged sticks as they tried to guide it into an openbacked truck.

Kate decided to make a run for it. She had only to sidle down the street, make a quick spurt for her front door, pull the string and she was safe. The drovers were getting nearer and nearer to the animal but he was not going to give in without a fight: he pawed the ground and snorted through both nostrils, his red-rimmed eyes rolling in panic. The redfaced drovers closed in slowly. Every time one of them took a step towards him, the bull tossed his head and bent it in his direction. Any second he would charge. As Kate reached her front door the animal swung around, fixed her with a wicked eye, rolled his head and prepared to gallop towards her. Her frantically searching fingers groped through the letterbox but the string had disappeared. She pounded on the door, screaming. The sharp edges of the panels cut through her knuckles, but the noise she made echoed hollowly through the empty house.

She turned in desperation and twisted the handle of the door beside her own. It opened easily, unexpectedly, and she fell through it into the long hall. She climbed to her feet and stood against the wall gasping for breath. Then she remembered a story her mother had told her of a bullock that came through the front door of her home on a fair day. It had run straight through the hall and had got wedged at the turn of the stairs where it remained all day. Any moment now the bull would paw its angry way into the hall. She raised a shaking hand and snibbed the door.

Then she moved further down the hall.

It was the entrance to the living accommodation of the pub next door. Nobody had lived above it for years and the hall had become a disreputable place which drunks fell into to urinate when the pub closed. It had always been a thorn in Harriet's side and she had often talked of reporting it to the Council and having it boarded up. Eventually she had decided that as they were leaving anyway it was hardly worth getting involved. It was better to pretend that it wasn't there. Harriet always passed it without a glance. Now Kate was standing in the middle of it in pitch blackness. Under her shoes something like wet sand grated. She lifted her foot and knew she was standing in a puddle. Nauseated, she stepped aside. She reached her hand across the wall in the darkness. It touched something warm and soft - another hand. As she screamed a black shadow detached itself from the corner. A man stepped in front of her. She almost gagged at the smell of his unwashed body close to her own, his greasy jacket brushed her face.

"Stop screaming."

His voice was soft, high-pitched, unpleasant. One hand held the back of her head close to his serge trousers while soft sweaty fingers kneaded her face.

"A little girl."

His voice was exultant, trembling with pleasures to come.

"Lost. You're lost aren't you? Come down here until I see you."

Still holding the back of her hair he stumbled her before him towards the back of the hall. Light filtered through a filthy skylight. The man was tall and thin. He leered at her, baring long yellow teeth in the semi-darkness. Kate looked up at him - recognised him. She stepped back and cowered against the filth-encrusted wall.

Billings stepped closer.

His breath was foul on her face as he bent down and slid his hand up the back of her jumper. Then he pressed her face close to him and she could feel the buttons of his jacket press against her cheekbone. The stench of unwashed flesh was almost unbearable. Now the hand slid down her back. To her horror, she felt it push through the elasticated waistband of her skirt. Down it went into the green interlock knickers with the large red patch her mother had sewn on them. Kate, mesmerised with fear, never made a sound.

"You like that, don't you?"

When she didn't answer he slid his hand out of her skirt and jerking her head back by the hair, he slapped her face.

"You little bitch. Stuck up like the rest of them."

Then he pulled her face close to him again. Kate felt herself gag and thought that she was going to be sick. Now he was stroking her face and whispering words, bad words.

"I won't touch you again, only if you let me."

Kate was silent. A terrible trembling was starting at the bottom of her spine.

"If I give you a penny?"

"No. Please no. I want to go home."

"Please, please." He ground his teeth in agony. "Just let me for a second. I won't hurt you."

He pulled her head back again and in the gloom he stared into her face. He started.

"Where do you live? I know your face."

Kate pointed to the wall behind him.

"In there."

"What?" His eyes darted to and fro. She knew he was scared. If she could only be brave, stop herself from trembling, stop herself from being sick.

"Does your mother know you're in here?"

She nodded, unable to speak.

"Where is she?"

"At our door." It was barely a whisper. "I lost my ball in here."

The trembling was worse now, her teeth were chattering.

"Your name?"

He was faltering now.

"Kate Regan."

He was convinced.

"She's the Protestant woman," he said.

She shook her head to deny that but could not speak. "Come here."

Now passion had gone and all was caution. He dragged her up three steps at the end of the hall and opened a broken door. Iron steps, the remains of an ancient fire escape, led down to a glass roof and from there to the ground far below. This must once have been the annex to the pub which Harriet had often told her about. In the early part of the century it had been a beergarden and the poshest place in town to visit. Now it was a rotting reminder of the past. Most of the panes of glass were missing and the frame of decaying wood sagged at the centre, heavy with pools of rainwater and rotting leaves.

Billings pushed her forward.

"If you ever tell anyone that you met me, I'll get you and throw you down there. Your bones will be broken and you'll never be found."

She shook her head to convince him she would never tell anybody.

An idea seemed to strike him. He leaned through the door and looked upwards.

"If you live next door that must be a window in your house?"

Kate looked up and recognized the heavy cream lace curtains of the landing window at the back of the house.

She nodded.

"If you tell anyone lies about me, I'll climb in there at night and get you. I have suction boots and can walk up walls."

"What kept you?" her mother said. "I've had your tea ready this hours. I was hanging clothes out the back and I thought I heard a knocking on the door but when I came in there was nobody there." She looked at Kate closely. "God daughter, what ails you, you look as if you've seen a ghost?"

"There was a wild bull charging around the street," Kate said.

"Is that why you're shaking all over?" Harriet laughed with scorn. "Dear me, but you're the timid wee thing. Thone was no bull that you saw. It was a poor oul' jaused cow they were taking to Burnhouse to make into dog meat."

* * *

Now Kate was afraid to go up the stairs after dark or to go out - even for the eggs. Although the War was over, eggs were still rationed but her mother's grocer was able to get her a half-dozen every week from his brother who was a farmer. They had to be collected from his home on Saturday nights, they couldn't be handed over in the shop in case they caused jealousy among the other customers. It was Kate's job to go for the eggs, the only time she was allowed out after dark. She had always loved going down the steep hill from her home to the lighted town below.

Now it was a nightmare.

She would walk in the middle of the road in case Billings would jump out of a gateway and pull her in. She would pass the old disused chapel with its strange gleaming lights and stare straight ahead. Here the wall was low and broken, the ground fell steeply away behind it.

Billings could lurk here and catch her ankle as she passed by. She would stand in the hall of the grocer's house, safe in the warmth and the light until Mrs Timoney would come out of her kitchen and hand her the bag of fresh brown eggs. Reluctantly she would step out into the night and hear the heavy door close behind her.

She would walk along the lighted town to find a safer way home. King Street was part of a ring road which ran around the old Cathedral on a plateau above the town. Three steep hills led up to it. Kate would walk to Wellington Street which was wide and well lit and climb happily enough but soon she would come to her own street, dark and narrow. Unseen things rustled in gateways as she passed. Sometimes from the corner of her eye she thought she could see the gleam of Billings' mad eyes.

She longed to tell her mother of her terror but Harriet seemed to be so pure and remote that she could never find the words or the moment.

At night the words he had whispered to her beat in her brain, rhyming like poetry.

She knew they were evil words and she willed herself not to think about them - it was a relief when they began to fade from her mind, but one night, somewhere between sleeping and waking, a creature which called itself *Dizzy Sense* appeared high on a wall in a corner of the room. *Dizzy Sense* knew the terrible words and mouthed them at her from the wall.

Harriet would laugh when she would see Kate run upstairs to the lavatory at night.

"You'll break your neck coming down them stairs," she would say.

Shortly after the incident with Billings, a concert was held in the Town Hall for a local charity. All the schoolchildren, Catholic and Protestant, were there. At the finale the cast came out and bowed to the audience. They were greeted with loud applause. The orchestra struck up with *God Save the King*. The pupils of the Protestant schools stood up as one, and with heads held high and heaving chests, pledged their loyalty to the King of England. The children of the Catholic schools remained seated, staring ahead in offended silence.

Behind Kate a seat creaked and somebody stood up.

She turned around and saw Barbara Sedgemore, the daughter of a British Army officer, standing to attention, alone in a sea of Catholics. She had come into Kate's class recently and was well liked by her classmates, although most of them could not understand how she could be the daughter of a British Army officer and a Catholic. To the Northern Ireland Catholic the two things seemed to be mutually exclusive. Ciara had also seen her and she glared towards her and turned back to Kate.

"Little bitch. How could she do a thing like that?"

"It's only Babs," Kate said, feeling something like admiration for the lone Nationalist. "She doesn't understand, she's new here and after all she is English."

She turned around again to smile at her - and spotted Billings sitting behind her.

He was seated at the back of the hall among the teachers and the few parents who had attended the concert. His eyes glittered in his thin face. He was looking straight over towards her. She turned away and sat drained and silent until the music was over and the curtain came down. She filed out quickly in the middle of the crowd, sick with fear. Now she didn't care who was Catholic or Protestant, she just wanted to be surrounded by people who would protect her.

"Will you leave me home girls?"

Ciara stood in a group of girls. Barbara, unconscious of her social gaffe, stood beside her. Kate looked towards Ciara pleadingly - she was a natural leader unconscious of her power, if she came with her the others would follow unquestioningly. She dithered while Kate prayed, then shook her head.

"No, I was told to be home for nine, it's nearly that now."

To prove her point the clock on the Catholic church chimed and began to strike the hour.

"C'mon, just a wee bit of the way."

But they were moving away from her, leaving her to go home alone.

"I can't, honestly, I'll see you tomorrow."

They turned in a body and went the other way.

Quickly, she walked through the town and turned up the steep hill to King Street. She arrived gasping for breath at the corner of the street. Here all was dark, narrow, empty of people.

She walked along, jumping at every sound.

Did she hear footsteps padding behind her? She couldn't be sure but she was too terrified to turn around and see. At last she reached her own front door and banged on it with her fists, gulping for air.

"Hold your horses," Harriet said opening the door. "Honestly, you're getting worse every day. What way is that to knock on your own front door? You'd think there was an army after you."

But Kate didn't care how much Harriet scolded.

I'm safe, she thought. He was there at the concert and he didn't get me.

* * *

The following morning when she arrived at school Ciara was waiting for her in the corridor, bursting with news.

"Did you hear about Barbara?"

"No, what?"

"Billings got her."

"How awful," Kate said, feeling nothing but relief that Barbara had been the victim and she had been spared.

"What happened?" she asked casually while the blood throbbed dangerously in her head.

Ciara selected a strand of straight hair and wound it carefully around her ear.

"After we left you we walked on down the town. We said goodbye to Barbara at the corner of her street, the rest of us went home together. Billings must have followed her because she was alone. He offered her half a crown if she would show him where Captain Madden lived."

He only offered me a penny, Kate thought.

"What happened?" she said aloud.

Her legs were trembling but her voice was smooth and innocent. Now she could almost smell Billings, could hear his vile suggestions but nobody must know that she too was tainted by him.

Ciara gave a sly wink.

"Nobody is talking but I asked Brigid what really happened to Babs."

Brigid was a girl from Donegal who helped Ciara's mother in the house. Although she was only fifteen she was a mine of information on forbidden topics.

"What did she say?"

Ciara leaned over and whispered.

"He done the deed."

They stared at each other, perplexed.

They soon got used to Barbara's empty chair. They knew she was in hospital but their teacher never asked them to visit her. Nor did she arrange to send her flowers from her classmates.

Billings was in jail.

One day, many weeks later, they came into the classroom in a laughing chatting group and saw Barbara sitting at her desk. She was, as always, beautifully dressed and as always her thick hair tumbled abundantly on her shoulders. But her face was thin and the eyes that looked towards them were bleak and humble.

"Hello Barbara."

"Hello."

Her mouth twitched nervously. They watched her covertly all morning. After lunch they went out to play in the playground. Their days of hopscotch and skipping were suddenly over, after the Summer holiday they would be going to Grammar school. Now they walked in sedate groups in the school yard. Barbara came out of the classroom behind them and stood shyly at the edge of the playground, her eyes on the ground.

Ciara hesitated as they passed her for the second time.

"I'm going over to ask Babs to join us, she should be here with us."

But Kate could not bear to be near Barbara now - Billings was everywhere around her. His foul breath was her sweet breath, his glittering green eyes her soft brown ones. His unwashed body was hers.

She pulled Ciara aside.

"She stood for *The King*. You can't forget a thing like that."

Ciara looked towards her and her mouth tightened with disapproval.

"I had forgotten about that."

They left her standing.

* * *

The sun went down. The sky remained light azure but the turret of the cathedral was black against it. The crows that had screeched through the evening were now silent, snug in their heavy nests in the old trees. Outside, the street was lonely and silent. Street lights flickered and came on, preparing for darkness.

Downstairs, Harriet raked the fire and slacked it down for the night.

The kettle hissed and spat.

In Kate's room shadows appeared in corners and silently eased themselves across the room towards her. Slowly the wardrobe became indistinct. She got out of bed, pulled the blinds closed and switched on the light. She could hear the rattle of the cup and saucer that her mother carried up the stairs.

"Careful, don't spill."

She stood by the bed uncertainly while Kate drank the tea.

"Well, I'm off to bed now."

"Oh, alright."

"Don't leave the light on too long."

"No, I'll put it out soon."

But Mummy, she said to her secret mother, I've seen Billings. He's out of jail and he's out there somewhere. He could pull the string on the front door and come in at night or he could come in through the landing window.

Harriet stood looking at her daughter, her face puzzled.

"Did you say something?"

"No."

"Goodnight now."

"Goodnight."

She put the light out and opened the blinds just before the street lights went out at eleven o'clock. She even slept for a while.

She was tugged awake as the Cathedral clock struck two. She lay wide awake, rigid and watchful. The night was still and silent. Why did the tassel of the blind tap against the window when there was no breeze and why did the brass door-handle rattle?

She slid down the bed and sat at the window. Moonlight silvered the night with an eerie light and turned the tips of the headstones in the graveyard to old bones. The pale moonlight gave a dignity to the old street that it did not have by day. In the semicircle of old houses topped by the Cathedral Kate could almost see the outline of the ancient City. But there was something else out there apart from the old Church and the Christianity it represented, something pagan and evil. She could feel it all around her, enveloping her, turning her to stone. She backed away from the window filled with a nameless terror, and with shaking hands opened the bedroom door.

She felt a rush of warm air as she stepped onto the landing. She stood for a moment and felt the house pulse and breathe around her. From the other room she could hear her mother snore gently as she slept. She padded along the warm linoleum to the bathroom which was right beside Harriet's bedroom. There was a light in the bathroom but when she came out and turned it off the house seemed to be more sinister than ever. The long landing corridor which led to her bedroom was bathed in milky moonlight. She looked down to where the Indian hung and could not face it.

She turned in the other direction and fumbled desperately for the handle to the door of her mother's bedroom.

* * *

They had only been in the house a few weeks when she had heard about the Indian. The children crowded around her when she was going to school and mimicked every word she spoke.

"Why do you say satchel? It's *schoolbag*."

"Don't youse live in the haunted house, the one where the blackie hung himself?"

"Nobody hanged themselves in our house."

"They did so, my mother says that nobody would live in that house but youse and that youse aren't real Catholics."

"Why not? We go to Mass."

"But there's no holy pictures on your wall and your grandfather is an oul' orange Billy."

Harriet was rolling out pastry, her lips moving as if in silent prayer when Kate rushed in to tell her.

"A blackman hanged himself here? No, I don't think so."

She stood thinking.

"But funny, I do remember an Indian family lived around here somewhere when I was young. We didn't know much about this part of the town, it was where all the millworkers lived. I never thought that

99

I'd be living here."

Her mouth drooped.

"Anyway there was this wee fat man, he always wore a dark suit and shiny patent shoes. I remember his shoes because he used to come around the doors with a case full of ribbons and things. Oul' dear shabby goods. When we would try to close the door, he'd push his foot in to hold it open. I haven't seen nor heard of him this years. Maybe he did kill himself here. I often think there's something strange about this house. It gives me the creeps. I often think that someone is standing behind me."

She shivered and turned around quickly.

"Not here. Upstairs. They said that he did it upstairs," Kate said.

"Sure there's nowhere upstairs he could have done it."

"Maybe from a picture rail?"

"Not at all," Harriet laughed. "Them wee spindly rails wouldn't hold your grandmother's 'Highland Cattle' pictures let alone thone big heavy Indian."

But Kate had his form now and she had to place him somewhere, as she did later with *Dizzy Sense* on the wall and Billings forever lurking in the long hall.

"The attic door on the landing?"

"Aye, I suppose he could have thrown a rope over a beam in the attic."

She was losing interest. "You're a funny wee girl, the things you think of."

*   *   *

Kate crept into the hot airless room and climbed in beside her.

Harriet was awake immediately, taut and listening.
Kate did not speak.

She almost felt her mother's shudder of revulsion
as she drew herself away and curled up, waiting.

"Mummy, are you awake?"

There was silence. Even her breathing had stopped.

Kate lay there, flooded with embarrassment and
humiliation.

She climbed out of the bed again and walked along
the dark landing. The door to the attic was outside
her bedroom. Now she could almost see the Indian
dangling from a rope. He swung gently backwards
and forwards, his body encased in a dark pinstripe
suit. His black pointed shiny shoes almost brushed
her face as she tripped and threw herself through her
bedroom door. She thought she heard him sigh
gently, the breath forever expelled from his body.

She climbed into her bed with her heart thumping
in her ears and hid her head under the blankets. At
last she dozed off, but with sleep came dreaming and
soon the staring eyes and thin face of *Dizzy Sense*
were grinning at her from the wall. She could waken
herself when she became very frightened. She lay
there in the dark room not daring to sleep again.
Gradually the black thinned and turned to grey. A
caw from the trees was followed by an answering
caw. Soon the air was filled with a raucous noise.

Down the street a door banged. Footsteps clacked
along the pavement, joined by other footsteps. The
workers, mostly women, were going to the early shift
at the mill. At last she could relax.

Her long watch was over.

She fell fast asleep.

When she woke up and saw the outline of the man against her window she thought for one wild moment her father was back and that she had only dreamed he was dead. She sat up in bed, laughing. Steele, sitting at the bottom of the bed, laughed back at her.

"Awake at last. That was some sleep, the room was shaking with your snoring."

"I don't snore."

He smiled.

"I came up to take a blood sample."

He laid his black bag on the bed and opened it. Quickly he assembled his equipment, his fingers moving deftly through the small bottles.

It's like watching my mother baking, Kate thought. She lays her ingredients out in the same orderly way.

He laid her arm across his knee. She could feel the rough tweed of his trousers and the warmth beneath. She squirmed with embarrassment.

"Sit still, it's hard enough to get a needle into your arm without you wriggling about. God but you've small veins."

He wiped her arm with spirit soaked in cotton wool, tidied his instruments away and closed his bag. Then he walked to the window and stood with his back to her, looking out. For a while he said nothing and behind him Kate could see the crows wheel around the turret of the old church. Through the open window came their vexed cries.

"Your recovery is very slow," he said without turning around.

"You should be up and about by now, I was thinking about you last night. Something seems to be hindering your progress."

"What?"

He shrugged.

"You tell me."

There was a silence.

"Your blood sedimentation rate is higher that it was when you came to bed."

"I have no control over that - you told me yourself it was a way of following the progress of some chronic infections such as TB ... by measuring the rate at which red blood cells fall to the bottom of a container ..."

Is that what he had told her when they were out yesterday? She wasn't sure, but he just said, "I know you have no direct control over it but I don't believe that the mind and the body are separate ... I think you are in a very anxious state and it's not helping your physical recovery. I saw how much you enjoyed yourself yesterday," he turned around, "I can't explain it Kate, but you were different out there. You were light and free. Then I saw you tense up again as you got near home - so I've decided to bring you for a wee jaunt as often as I can. I've taken another blood sample and will continue to take them at regular intervals. If the rate begins to drop, we'll know that we're on the right track ..."

"When does the treatment start?"

"The sooner the better, I think."

He smiled towards her, a conspiratorial smile and suddenly, blindingly, Kate could see what her mother meant when she called him handsome.

"Would you like a breath of fresh air after lunch?"

Her heart gave a leap of joy.

"So soon?"

"I have a few hours free. I'm going fishing. If you'd

like to come you could sit in the car and read a book.
I'll call at three."

Harriet lent Kate her jigger. She came into the
bedroom brushing invisible specks from the sleeves.
It had hung in her wardrobe for years, forever
waiting for the big occasion that never came to pass.

"You may as well wear it," she said in answer to
Kate's protests. "God knows when I'll ever get a
chance."

It was a red muted check, straight at the front with
a swing back. It fitted nicely over her red polonecked
sweater. She walked to the mirror and turned the
collar up, then she put her hands deep into her
pockets and pouted her lips as the film stars did in
the American magazines that Martha Grey had
brought up to her on her last visit.

Martha's sister had married a Yank and had gone
to live in America. Now she sent all the glossy film
magazines home to her young sister.

"My mother says you can keep them," she had said,
dumping the pile of dog-eared books on the bed,
while looking embarrassed because she knew that
Kate was sensitive enough to realise that the reason
Mrs Grey did not want the books back was that they
might be infected with tuberculosis. Kate guessed
that Harriet with her puritanical upbringing would
not approve of her reading the magazines so she hid
them under the mattress and only took them out to
read late at night when she was sure her mother had
gone to bed.

Harriet turned around and saw something in her
daughter's posturing that made her uneasy.

"Take your hands out of the pockets of that jigger.
And stop twisting your face like an eejit."

She looked towards Kate with beetling brows.

"What's a jigger anyway? That word went out with the Indians. A jigger indeed." Kate tittered.

Harriet banged the door as she left the room.

Steele's car swayed gently over the dry wheeltracked clay. Again he had stopped at a bridge where the main road spanned a valley. Far below the river gurgled among the trees.

"I'll be down there, Kate. You can listen to the wireless or read, whatever you like. If you get fed up sitting in the car you can stand at the bridge for a wee while. But not for long, that wind still has a bite to it. If you need me, call."

He went to the boot of the car and began to change into wellingtons and collect his tackle. Kate rolled the window down. Beside her, Steele stood balancing on one foot, folding the ends of his trousers to fit into his boots. He sang an operatic tune in an embarrassingly loud and tuneless voice. That's from *Carmen*, she thought, and felt proud to have recognised it. She turned and saw his stockinged feet and with revulsion a flash of white leg covered with thick black hair. Like an animal, she thought, and stared in front of her, rigid with embarrassment. As long as she could remember, Steele had been one of the Establishment figures, as right as God. The priests of the town, the doctors and the teachers minded people's bodies, their minds, their souls. Steele's hairy legs shocked Kate as much as if she had seen a nun coming into the classroom wearing rouge and lipstick or a priest suddenly begin to dance on the altar. He

left her with a jaunty wave and slid down the steep
hill at the side of the bridge. Now Kate was alone in
the car.

She closed her eyes and felt the heat of the sun on
her face. The leather seat was soft and comfortable.
She leaned over and switched on the radio.

I'm a spoiled rich girl, she thought, waiting for my
father who has gone fishing.

You touch my fingertips and my heart is aglow,
You bend to kiss my lips and I can't let you go ...
sang the voice of Hoagy Carmichael. Kate joined in
although the sentiments of the song were
meaningless to her. She had never been in love but
she knew all the modern songs since Harriet had
puffed upstairs with the huge wireless and set it in
solitary glory beside her bed.

Steele was a long time down at the river. Kate
examined her face in the mirror above the driving
wheel, poked through the glove compartment, looked
up and down the blacktarred road, turned the radio
on and off then climbed carefully out of the car. The
air was warm, heavy with the smell of blossom, a
trick day early in May. She stood beside the bridge
and again felt the stillness and peace. She had always
been familiar with the countryside, half a mile
outside the town in any direction led straight to the
heart of it. Like all the children in the town she had
spent her childhood fishing for spricks with jam jars,
out gathering mushrooms in the early mornings or
picking primroses in the late afternoons. But that had
been snatched from her almost two years ago and
now suddenly she was plunged back into the middle
of it.

It was like being born again.

Her senses were heightened and everything around her was imbued with a piercing beauty. Her thighs caressed the rough granite of the bridge, she could feel the coldness of the long coarse grass as it waved around her legs. She leaned over the bridge and watched the foreshortened figure of Steele far below as he threw an invisible line into the river. Suddenly she was swept with a wave of feeling for him which startled her in its intensity. She wanted to rush down to the river, to touch his rough jacket, his hands, his hair. She wanted to circle his broad shoulders with her arms, lay her head on his chest.

She was stunned by the suddenness and depth of her emotion and she stood by the bridge breathing heavily, gripping the sides of the stone slabs, trying to control her trembling legs. She had known Steele since she came to the town as a young girl. Since she had become ill he had called to see her at least once a week, now almost every day. He was concerned that her health was not improving as quickly as he had hoped and he kept an eye on her. She in turn had come to trust him as a friend, looked forward to his calls. But she never had any romantic feeling towards him, she thought of him as someone in her mother's age group. Now, suddenly, her feelings had changed. Her mind was in turmoil. She was barely aware of the car which came around the corner, slowed down and pulled in beside her. The door opened and a long elegant leg appeared followed by a body as slim and fashionable as a male model's.

Petie Nixon, the breadman, stood beside her.

"Hello Kate, I thought it was you, I haven't seen you for ages. What are you doing in this neck of the woods? Isn't that Dr Steele's car?"

He leaned over the bridge. "Oh, there he is down there."

He looked at her shrewdly. "Did you come out here with him?"

She shrugged, embarrassed. Where there was no guilt yesterday, there was guilt now.

"Yes."

He looked at her, puzzled.

"Are you his secretary?"

"No, I've been ill, he brought me out for some air."

"Sorry to hear that, I didn't know you weren't well, although I haven't seen you coming from school lately, come to think of it ... nothing serious, I hope?"

"I have tuberculosis."

Petie gulped and looked into the distance.

"They say consumption can be cured now, there's a new medicine out called penicillin ... it's made from a mould, I think. There was an article about it in the *Reader's Digest*. Ask your man about it," he nodded towards Steele. "He might be able to get some for you."

"He told me about the miracle drugs, but I don't need them. I'm not positive, I only need rest."

"That's great," Petie said, not believing her. "I suppose you're up in the Sanatorium?"

"No, I attend outpatients for x-ray."

"Just as well, the only way out of that place is feet first. I should know, my pal Joe Martin snuffed it in the San." He leaned one elbow on the bridge and crossed his long legs - every movement of his lean muscular body was graceful. "He coughed up buckets of blood the morning he croaked it ... buckets of it."

He looked over towards her.

"Watch him." He jerked his head towards the river

below.

"What do you mean?"

He sniggered and put his finger along the side of his nose. Then he winked at her slowly.

Down below they heard a faint sound. They leaned forward on the bridge and saw Steele jumping up and down waving his arms.

"He seems to be waving at us, I wonder what he wants."

"Maybe he's caught a fish."

They watched him break down the rod and run towards them, scrabbling at the clumps of grass to pull himself up the steep sides of the bank. Petie walked over to give him a hand over the ditch and onto the side of the road but Steele knocked his hand aside. His face went red with exertion and anger. He glared over at Kate.

"Get into that car."

She slunk past him and climbed into the car, her heart thumping. What had she done?

Petie stood, lean and relaxed, watching them with interest, looking like an advertisement for smart fishing gear. Beside him Steele looked squat and almost paunchy. Petie smiled goodbye to her, showing white even teeth.

"Cheerio Doc."

Steele ignored him and jumped into the car. Petie stepped nimbly aside as the big car lurched forward, barely missing his toes. Kate sat silent and miserable as they drove fast along leafy lanes. She glanced towards Steele but he was hunched over the wheel scowling. She stared quickly in front of her. At last he slowed the car down and they bumped into a grassy clearing. They had moved quite a distance along the river and she could see it through the trees, a gleaming band of silver.

"Is this a better place for fishing?"

He did not answer. He stared at the windscreen with a set sulky face. She gulped and stared silently in front of her. She was very sensitive to people's moods. Making a thoughtless remark or bringing the wrong schoolfriend home had sometimes condemned her to weeks of silence from her mother. She had learned to be careful of what she said, to see every friend through her mother's eyes before she asked them to call for her.

She knew that Petie was the cause of the trouble now, that her obvious friendship with him had offended Steele. It occurred to her that maybe Steele was a snob and didn't like to think the man who delivered his bread shared his favourite hobby. But she knew this was not true. Everything she had ever heard about him pointed to a different type of character, to a man who would have despised petty snobbery and who would always judge people by their worth.

She wondered if it was the fact that Petie was a Catholic going with a Protestant girl. She knew that many of the Protestant people in the town resented it. Petie and his girl hadn't married and he still squired her to the weekend dances. She looked buxom now, and her lovely fair hair had a brassy dyed look but she had not taken the final step that would cut her off from her own people for all time. Steele's voice cut across her thoughts.

"Did you ever court him?"

'Coort', he said, in the rough local accent.

She stared at him in amazement.

"No."

"I would imagine that a young girl like you would find him very attractive."

"Oh yes, he's goodlooking." Nobody could deny Petie his good looks. "But he's old."

"Old?" his voice was strained. "How old would you say he is?"

"At least thirty."

"Thirty?" he gave a bitter laugh. "Anyway, how do you know him so well?"

"I've always known Petie ... he delivered bread to the Convent, he was usually leaving as I was coming out from school for lunch and he would give me a lift home. He would stop the van here and there and I would run out and leave the bread on the window-sills of houses."

She thought of Petie, dry and warm inside the van while she ran back and forward in the wind and the rain leaving unwrapped loaves on damp window-sills.

"Sometimes he'd give me a threepenny bit for helping."

She could almost feel the sharp edges of the threepenny piece cut into her hands.

"I never told my mother."

"If you associate with people like him you can't come out with me again."

A small cloud came over the sun. She shivered.

"I don't associate with him. Anyway what's wrong with him?"

"He's a spiv."

"What's a spiv?"

He looked at her quickly and didn't answer. He uses words like my mother uses, she thought. 'Spiv' and 'jigger' and she knew that he would probably call women 'broads'

Suddenly his mood changed and he smiled.

"Look, we'll forget about it and go for a walk and don't worry, I'll look after you."

The cloud passed over and the sun shone brightly as they left the car and walked along the field towards the river.

"Do you like the country?"

"I love the country, I've missed it terribly since I became ill."

"Good, if you're going to spend time with me you will have to like the country."

Spend time with me, spend time with me. Her heart sang. Steele stopped suddenly.

"What's that?"

Kate looked at the ground thinking he had seen a watch or a purse. But there was nothing on the cropped ground except a dark mound. She averted her eyes ... really he could not be pointing to ...

"I said what's that?"

When she looked again Steele's shoe was still pointing to the embarrassing heap.

"A rabbit has ..." her voice trailed off.

"Not a rabbit, a hare."

He gripped her arm lightly above the elbow and guided her along, pacing his steps with hers. The slightest pressure of his hand on her arm set her heart beating so loud that she looked at him in alarm thinking that he must be aware of it. Something had happened her today at the bridge, she had fallen in love with Steele and she could never tell him.

"When you walk through the town," he was saying "hold your head high but when you walk in the country look at the ground. There is so much to be seen. If you learn to recognize droppings you will know what animals are in the area and how recently they have been around." He tightened his hold on her arm and pulled her closer to him.

"You know Kate, sometimes when people have been ill for a long time they become engrossed with themselves and their sickness, they look inward all the time and that's not healthy."

"Are you saying that I'm like that?"

"I think that you're very tense and anxious. Relax, forget about yourself and look around you. Take everything in, let your mind absorb it, then when you can't sleep at night bring it all back. Now look at that field rising in front of us and tell me what you see."

"I see a flock of sheep."

"Close your eyes and tell me how many sheep you saw."

"About seven ... I think."

"Ewes?"

"Yes, they were ewes."

"And there were no lambs."

She shook her head.

"Anything else? Trees, bushes?"

"A big tree in the middle of the field."

"What kind of a tree was it?"

"A blue tree," she said laughing.

"Now open your eyes and look again."

There were three ewes in the field, one had twin black lambs, they stood side by side like knitted toys at a fair. Two other lambs, each bleating beside its mother, had white curly bodies with black feet and black faces, as though some mighty knitter had run out of wool and improvised.

"Blackfaced lambs," Steele said.

What Kate had taken for a tree was a stationary tractor, now it chugged slowly across the horizon trailed by a flock of white gulls under a blue sky. From where she stood she could hear their faint cries.

"Look."

Steele pulled her over by the hand.

In a patch of grass among the yellow gorse was a hare. He stared at them for a few seconds with velvet eyes. Kate held her breath and watched him. His nose twitched nervously, scenting humans, scenting danger and suddenly he bounded away and disappeared into the undergrowth.

She gasped and looked at Steele.

"They only let you have a peep at them occasionally but when they do it makes all the stalking worthwhile."

Chapter Three

In the weeks that followed Kate found that Steele had a happy nature. He always sang as he drove along in the car, he told her jokes and hair-raising stories about his student days. One day in June sitting beside him in the car she began to sing a song she had learned in the school choir.

"*Hoven, hoven gory o go*
gory o go
gory o go."

Steele looked at her in surprise

"I've never heard you sing before."

She flushed. She hadn't realised that she had been singing.

"C'mon, don't stop now. *Hoven, hoven gory o go.*" he sang. "*I've lost my darling baby o,*" they sang together as they bowled along the green countryside. They were driving home through sunsoaked lanes, heat vibrated from the bonnet of the car as it slid smoothly over bubbling tar roads. Kate watched Steele, covertly glancing at his face when she thought he wouldn't notice: his eyes were dark blue and fringed with thick black lashes, his skin was dusky and his hair curled on the back of his neck. She wondered what he was thinking about. He seemed so calm. Once again she had an almost insane desire to touch him, to feel the roughness of his tweed jacket against her skin, to stroke the back of his neck. The thought horrified her. She clenched her hands into tight fists and felt her face go red with shame.

"Kate, are you poor?"

The question stunned her, brought her back to her senses. So Steele thought they were poor and was kind to her only because he pitied her. He had noticed that she had only one skirt and that she wore her mother's jigger. Kate had never thought of her mother and herself as poor. For years she had watched Harriet scrimp and save. Nothing was ever wasted or thrown away. Sheets were patched and then turned as the material in the centre wore thin, her dresses which were made with a hem were let down until they had false hems to make them last yet another year. Unused bread was husbanded carefully to make bread puddings and a marrow bone was always simmering on the back of the stove to make stock for soup. Left-over potatoes reappeared on the table as potato bread, the trimmings of pastry from the apple tarts were pressed into service as pie crusts.

Every Tuesday when Harriet collected her Widow's Pension, she was able to put two pounds into her Post Office account. Laughingly they called it their escape money. When they had enough money they would close the front door of King Street forever and go back to England.

Then they would live again.

But in the early fifties everyone lived as carefully as they did, the forced frugality of the War years was not far behind them. The poor were different. They came to school infrequently, had runny noses, and nits in their hair. When the school nurse came around every year and everybody had their heads examined they were given warning letters to bring home to their parents. They wore odd unmatched clothes, heavy boots in Summer and canvas slippers in Winter.

Steele turned sideways to look at Kate and turned again when he saw her distraught face. He frowned.

"Look, you're far too sensitive. Everything I say seems to devastate you. I asked if you were poor. So what if you are? I'm poor. You should see me hiding when I see my bank manager."

"But you have a bank manager," Kate said. "A big car, a big house."

He smiled across at her. "And a big wife."

He ruminated, tapping the steering wheel.

"The thing is that I don't know much about your family circumstances."

She told him about her father and young brother being killed during the War. He listened in silence, showing no emotion.

"So my father is dead," her lips trembled.

He shrugged.

"You have a mother who cares about you. Think of the children who lost both parents in the War."

She felt slightly piqued at his callous remark. She felt little emotion now at her father's death. She had been very young when she left England and her memories of him were growing dim but the story of how he had died had been told and retold. It was honed almost to perfection and until now had never failed to draw exclamations of sympathy.

"You said your mother was at home here, when your father was killed. Is she a native of this town? I thought I knew everyone here but I can't place her."

Kate shrank back in her seat and her voice was almost inaudible.

"Her maiden name was Menary."

"Menary, Menary? The only Menary I know is Tom Menary the builder and a bad black get he is."

"He's my mother's father."

Steele looked at her and his mouth dropped open.

"But he's ..."

Kate knew what he had stopped himself from saying.

"My father was a tradesman, a Catholic from the Republic. As far as I know he came up to work for Menary and ran off with my mother."

"They always say that Menary wouldn't give a Catholic a crust of bread never mind employ one."

"Maybe he did employ the odd one before that but none since."

Suddenly Steele began to laugh with real amusement.

"Well Kate, you really surprise me. So that canting hypocrite is your grandfather."

Grandfather.

The word meant close family ties, loving and caring. It hardly described Kate's relationship to her mother's father. Once when she had just read *Heidi* she saw Menary going into his office in French Street. She waited outside until he came out then sidled over to him and smiled, hoping that, like Heidi, her sweet innocence would melt a heart of stone. Menary stopped, obviously puzzled and glanced towards her, then with a start bent close and looked into her face. For a moment Kate stared into her mother's green eyes. Then he drew back from her. She saw him bare his teeth in a snarl and she recognised the naked hatred on his face. She shrank from him, terrified. After that her legs would tremble when she saw him. She would do anything to avoid meeting him - often dashing onto the road and weaving dangerously through cars if she saw him approach. Now she told Steele about her encounter - the first time she had ever talked about it.

Steele shrugged it off.

"He's no loss to you, forget him. He doesn't hate you because you are you - he knows nothing about you. No, he hates you because of the shape of your nose, the colour of your eyes, because you must in some ways look like your father, the man who took his daughter away from him. When you realise that you'll feel better about yourself."

Kate could feel her spirits rising. Steele was right, she thought, Menary was nothing to her. In future she would walk tall when she met him, she would never skulk away again.

"I've met people like Menary, they thrive on bigotry and hatred, there are too many of them in Ulster." He turned around to her, driving the car slowly. "They haven't changed their ideas in three hundred years, probably because we've been fairly isolated here ..."

"They're remnants of small Scottish sects originally converted by John Knox." So Harriet had once told her.

"You've obviously studied your history, you know what I'm saying. You can see why he would look on you with fear and hatred. Your father a Free State Catholic?"

Steele began to laugh gently.

"To Menary you would be a child of Satan. "

But you're a Protestant too, she thought. Surely you all feel the same way about Catholics?

As if he heard her, he said,

"There is very little common ground between a mild Church of Ireland man like me and a rabid Evangelist like Menary."

He was silent for a while then he said,

"I remember there was a son, Billy Menary, a quiet chap. Of course he hadn't much choice with that man for a father."

"He lives in Ballymena," Kate said.

"Then there were two or three goodlooking daughters, but none of the lads would go sniffing around that house - thone oul' preacher would have blown your head off with a shotgun." He stopped suddenly, as though he remembered who he was talking to.

"Your mother couldn't be happy in a place like King Street. The people there are the other side of the coin, extreme, narrow-minded bigoted Catholics who wouldn't forget for one moment that she was the daughter of Menary. How did she end up in a place like that?" he asked after a moment.

"When we were stranded here during the War, she went to the Town Clerk for a house - she had gone to school with him. The only council house available was that one in King Street, so he gave it to her. There were fifty four in for the key," she added proudly.

It had always seemed to her a measure of the Town Clerk's respect for her mother that he had chosen her from so many.

"He always had a wee notion of me," Harriet had said once when Kate marvelled at their luck in getting a house.

"Would you not have married him?" Kate had asked. "He must have been very rich."

"I wouldn't have liked him to touch me," Harriet said, her mouth making a moue of distaste. "He had a withered hand."

But Steele was not impressed.

"Cyril Nixon was always an eejit. It was madness dumping her in a place like that. She would have been far better off to get away from this town altogether. A woman in her situation is neither fish nor fowl here."

Neither fish nor fowl. One of Harriet's own expressions.

"In all fairness to the people in King Street, I think they tried to make friends with her in the beginning but when she kept her distance they resented it. She thinks the people in the street watch us and talk about us, that's why she hardly ever goes out and keeps her curtains drawn all the time."

He looked at her sharply then shrugged.

"She's not my patient so I can't help her and they probably do talk about her. Even without her problems it would be easy to become paranoid in a street like that."

"The funny thing is that she's a devout Catholic, convinced that she belongs to the one true Church. She received her instruction from a Jesuit in England."

"She probably spent most of her youth crawthumping. Has any of her religious fervour rubbed off on you?"

"No."

Steele laughed.

"Well, you're honest ... I hope you don't think that I am being nosy. I have a reason for asking you about your family circumstances. You may be entitled to a disability payment."

"Money for being sick?"

"Well yes, you're over sixteen and chronically ill. If it's there you may as well get it."

He reached into an inside pocket and drew out a form.

"Get your mother to fill that up and I'll sign it and get if off in the post, you may be lucky."

When they drew up at the front door he braked the car.

"Are you interested in birds?"

"Birds?" He had a disconcerting habit of jumping from one subject to another.

"You love the country so much. I thought that I could teach you more about them. Birds are my speciality really - a fascinating hobby."

"I love birds."

"Good, I noticed that you didn't seem to have much to read but a few dull oul' poetry books."

She felt a stab of disappointment. She loved her poetry books, and had passed many of the long hours in her room reading her favourite poems.

"I'll bring some books up tomorrow. I'll call around two - we're going to Donegal."

* * *

"Donegal?" said Harriet. "You'll have to cross the Border. It's somewhere in the South."

"I wonder what it's like."

"Like any other Free State town, full of pubs and tinkers," said Harriet, who had never crossed the Border in her life.

Steele was late. Kate, dressed and ready to go, walked like a caged animal from one window to the other, and when his car finally turned into the street and slowed to a halt below the two windows she flung herself down the stairs.

"I thought you were supposed to be taking things easy," Harriet frowned her disapproval from the chair beside the fire.

But Kate barely had time to listen to her. She hurried through the front door and slammed it shut. She tried to open the door of the car but it wouldn't budge so she bent down and tapped the window to ask Steele to unlock the door. A woman, sitting beside Steele in the passenger seat, stared out at her. He gestured to the back door. She opened it and climbed in.

"Well Kate, how are you feeling today. Pamela this is Kate, the wee girl I've told you so much about. Kate, my wife Pamela."

Mrs Steele turned, gave Kate a brief absentminded smile then continued her conversation with her husband. Steele switched the engine on and they sped out of the street and down one of the hills which led to the Convent. Flocks of girls converged on the school gates. It was almost two years since she had walked these roads, talked of Shelley and the local boys. Would she ever be part of their world again? Probably not, she thought. There was Ciara sauntering along with the girl who lived beside her, Mary Trimble. She banged the window at them, waved frantically and beat her breast.

"It's me, it's me."

But as the car flew past she saw them through the back window shading their eyes and looking after them in puzzlement. Steele drove almost dangerously fast along the bumpy country roads. Kate, sitting in the middle of the back seat, was bounced around as they went over hillocks. They took a corner sharply and she fell forward and bumped her nose on the seat in front. Nobody appeared to notice. With streaming eyes she moved over and clung to the armrest of the car. From the front came the sound of relaxed inconsequential conversation from Steele and Pamela. Occasionally she heard them laugh. She couldn't hear what they were saying. In the back of the car she felt lonely and forgotten.

If I opened the door and jumped out they wouldn't even notice, she thought.

At last they stopped alongside a prefabricated building. Mrs Steele put her hand into the glove compartment and drew out a booklet.

"Customs, God damn them" Steele said to her in the back and taking the proffered booklet jumped out and disappeared into the hut. In the back Kate tossed opening gambits of conversations through her mind.

It's a beautiful day, isn't it? No, it was cloudy. She

remained silent. Mrs Steele, who looked completely relaxed and who obviously felt no obligation to talk to Kate, stared silently in front of her until her husband returned. As they travelled further into the Republic the road became narrower and even bumpier, the land became stony and marshy. They passed through small towns which were almost identical to each other: one wide main street, flanked with small plaster houses and dull brown shops. They didn't look very different to the small towns in Northern Ireland, not to Kate anyway, but they did to the Steeles.

"Look at how badly maintained the houses are," said Mrs Steele. "I went into that butcher shop once and it was so full of bluebottles that I had to run out."

Steele laughed. "Their standards of hygiene leave a lot to be desired."

Kate knew that Protestants always said unjustified and nasty things about the Republic because under the guidance of De Valera the Republic had maintained a neutral role during the War. She thought of Brigid, the Donegal girl who did all the work for Ciara's mother. She was the most hardworking girl Kate had ever seen and kept Ciara's home spotless while Ciara's mother spent her days visiting her friends.

"That's not fair," she said from the back of the car but her voice was a whisper against the noise of the engine and nobody heard her. As they came to the outskirts of Donegal town they pulled into the side of the road to let drovers pass them with their cattle.

"They're fine looking beasts," said Mrs Steele.

"Hmm, riddled with tuberculosis, most of them." said Steele. "There's a big education programme

going on warning the people about drinking
unpasteurised milk - but is difficult to convince them
that the milk is dangerous, especially in country
places where it was always part of their diet.
Consequently children with bovine TB are a common
sight."

"Have I bovine TB?" Kate asked from the back of
the car.

"No, it affects the bones."

They stopped in the main street.

"Pam, isn't that where you get your Bewley's
coffee? I'll nip over and get it for you ..."

"I'll go myself, I want to stretch my legs."

"Be careful, dear."

When Mrs Steele got out of the car, Kate saw that
she was pregnant. She wouldn't have noticed it
except for her mother's remark. They both watched
her as she walked slowly towards the shops. Then
Steele sat back and switched the radio on.

"If they made me a King, I'd still be a slave to you
If I had everything I'd turn on my knees to you."

The voice of the crooner was smooth and
insinuating. Is this what married love was, what
Steele and his wife felt for each other? He turned
around with a smile, remembering Kate.

"You're very quiet. Are you enjoying the spin? I
suppose you're wondering why I brought you along."

"Well, I was ..."

"We're going to visit some friends now. Alan and
Joanne Greene. I worked with Alan in the Adelaide in
Dublin, he's a Consultant now in a Sanatorium in
Donegal - he's an expert on the treatment of
tuberculosis."

He put his hand over hers on the back of the seat.

"Do you mind if I discuss your case history with him?"

Kate was alarmed.

"Will he examine me?"

"No, of course not. You're so tense, you're holding on to that seat like a vice." He disengaged her fingers one by one as he spoke. "Don't worry, I won't embarrass you, it's just that there are some unusual features ... I'd like to discuss them with him. There'll be no need for him to talk to you at all."

"Does he know I'm coming?"

"Yes, I rang him last night. Don't worry, you'll be made welcome, any friend of mine ..."

As Mrs Steele came towards them Kate was able to see her properly for the first time. She was small and slight with a pale narrow face and straight fair hair, her blue eyes were slightly protuberant like her husband's, but not as dark, not as attractive. Kate knew she had never seen her before but felt that she recognised her from somewhere, the cast of her features was strangely familiar. She was very like somebody she knew. With a shock she realised it was herself.

"Well what kind of coffee did you get?" she heard Steele say as he got out and opened the door for her.

"I got the French roast," she said as she sat into the car. "The bean is very dark, very aromatic."

"You know I prefer the Brazilian," Steele said irritably.

She turned to Kate.

"Do you like coffee?"

"Yes."

"What kind do you like?"

"Irel."

Why did she play the fool when she was no fool?
She saw them exchange fleeting glances of
amusement as they drove away.

* * *

Alan Greene's face was as craggy as the barren rocks
around him, his skin raw from the cutting Atlantic
winds. They were standing outside the gate of his
large modern house where Steele had parked the car.

"Leave it there Robby, we'll sneak down to
Murphys for a jar later," Kate heard him say in a low
voice.

"You hoor," Steele said laughing, "You never
change."

He walked before them into the house, a battered
corduroy jacket hanging from a frame so thin and
stooped that Kate thought he must often be mistaken
for one of his tubercular patients. At the front door he
stopped and ushered them in.

"Joanne," he called "these gets are here at last." He
turned to them.

"You'd better be hungry, this woman has been
buzzing around like a blue-arsed fly since she heard
you were coming."

Mrs Green came through a door from the kitchen
and stood for a moment looking at them, her face
beaming with pleasure. She was a tall, almost
statuesque woman with a substance that her husband
lacked. She walked over to Pamela first, put her arms
around her and kissed her with affection.

"Oh God, you're still such a fragile wee thing, you
always make me feel like a big horse."

"You are a big horse," said Steele coming over and

kissing her fondly on both cheeks. From behind, Kate was outraged to see his hand slide down to give her bottom a friendly squeeze.

"Here, enough of that," she said goodhumouredly giving him a swipe of the tea-towel in her hand. "Pam will you try to keep this man of yours under control."

She was introduced to Kate and gave her a brief firm handshake, for a moment Kate was looking directly into clear no-nonsense eyes.

"We didn't expect dinner," Pamela Steele said as they were ushered into the diningroom. She turned to her husband. "Robert, look at the trouble Joanne has gone to." She turned to Joanne, "we should have arrived out of the blue and surprised you."

"Well, I don't know about the rest of you but a good feed is just what I need, I'm starving," said Steele.

"Now that's the way to talk, the lads have been working in France since May and I've nobody to cook for, besides Teasie Boyle came in to help me ... now sit down everyone."

Kate took her seat and glanced quickly at her place setting, where there was a dazzling display of cutlery.

Where do I start, she thought with rising panic.

Oh God, is that small knife for fruit or is it for fish?

She felt calmer when she remembered Harriet telling her that when in doubt, start at the outside and work inwards. To be on the safe side she waited until everyone else had started then lifted the spoon at the outside of her plate and began to enjoy her soup. Don't sup it, she remembered Harriet saying, you must never make a noise when you're having soup. The Greenes were obviously well used to entertaining guests. Joanne sat beside her husband who was at the head of the table and managed to take part in a lively conversation while holding plates out for the meat he carved, passing them around, and bringing hot food to the table. As they ate, the conversation ebbed and flowed, the atmosphere was relaxed and friendly, these were people who knew each other well and were at ease in each other's company.

"You were a wise man to marry your theatre sister," Steele put his arm around Joanne as she filled his glass with wine. "You two certainly know how to operate as a team."

Joanne pulled away from him and moved to Kate, held the bottle over her glass and looked at him.

He shook his head.

"No, so she doesn't drink."

"How are things in the North since the National Health Service ... did Bevan do the medical profession a favour or not?" Alan Greene was asking Steele.

"Well, it's still hard to earn a crust with three GPs in one small town, all breathing down each other's throats..."

"The Health Service is the best thing that ever happened, Robert, you have to admit it," Pamela Steele said. "At least you're paid now for your calls."

"I suppose it's alright," Steele said without enthusiasm.

"Do you ever regret leaving Dublin?"

"If you remember, Alan, he couldn't get a job with any of the local health authorities," Pamela Steele said with a touch of bitterness.

"Is that because you were a Protestant?" Joanne Greene asked him wide-eyed.

"No, because I couldn't speak Irish," Steele said,

laughing. "I loved Dublin, we had some crack, hadn't we?" he said looking at the other man. Then he winked at him. "But then I didn't have the ball and chain in those days."

You look like a horse.

The ball and chain.

Kate, who was not used to socialising in mixed company or to being in men's company at all, thought that the women seemed to be denigrated. That was one of the things about being taught by nuns, she thought, they gave you a sense of respect for womanhood - but maybe she was being sensitive.

"I taught in Dublin for a while and I thought that I would never get out of it," Pamela Steele said. "The conditions that some of the people lived in were appalling ... children were dying like flies with gastro-enteritis and diphtheria ..."

Alan Greene turned to her.

"Yes Pam, that's all true but there are some great things happening now. We have the miracle drugs and a campaign to educate the public about hygiene ... which means cleaning up the sources of infection, like infected milk, dirty utensils." He turned to Steele. "You should see the new hospitals and the ones that are under construction at the moment, they're among the best in Europe - we have nearly six thousand beds for TB patients alone." His sparse brown hair was standing straight up on his head, he waved a spoon to emphasise the thrust of his conversation. "The death rate for tuberculosis has dropped from one hundred and twenty three per hundred thousand in 1947 to seventy three per hundred thousand in 1951, all after Noel Browne became Minister for Health."

And when he had done all that you crucified him,

Kate wanted to say. Over the past year or so Steele had always talked to her about the controversy raging over the 'Mother and Child' scheme. He had encouraged her to read the newspapers to form her own opinions. Now he was looking at her across the table, willing her to introduce it as a natural progression of the conversation.

"C'mon, you can do it," his eyes were saying. Here she would be on sure ground, she could argue each point with the best of them. But she was mute, the solitary years had changed her. She realised that she had a long way to go before she could relax with people again.

She looked for a spoon to eat her pudding and saw that she had nothing at her place but a dinner knife. What had she done with her spoon? She couldn't remember. It should have been easy to ask for another one, once it wouldn't have cost her a thought but now she couldn't do it. Her heart began to thump painfully and the old feeling of panic returned. People were still talking around her. Everyone had noticed the dreadful *faux pas* of course but they were too polite to say anything. Her face grew crimson and she hung her head.

Opposite her Robert Steele's spoon fell with a thump onto the floor.

"No, sit where you are, I can struggle out to the kitchen for a spoon." he said to Joanne. On the way back he passed Kate's place and dropped a spoon beside her.

With relief Kate began to eat her pudding. She looked across, caught Steele's eye and smiled her gratitude. As she looked away she saw that Alan Greene was watching her - a thoughtful expression on his face.

* * *

"How do you like your coffee?" Mrs Greene asked Kate later in the drawing room as she poured the thick dark liquid into small cups.

"*Au lait,*" Kate said remembering her school French.

The words cracked through the room like a pistol shot. It was the first time she had spoken since she had arrived at the house. Her voice was too loud in the quiet room. Everybody turned around and looked at her in surprise. Joanne Greene stood with the coffee pot poised in mid air.

"Did somebody say *olé*?"

Steele stood up.

"C'mon Alan, we'll go down to the hotel and have a pint for old times' sake."

The women protested.

"For heaven's sake, Robert," said Pamela "Why are you always so restless? Alan has all the drink you want here."

But Alan Greene was on his feet.

"I think that Robert is like myself - he must have the sawdust under his feet."

The men were heading to the door, one behind the other, smirking like schoolboys.

Pamela's voice tinkled with laughter and annoyance.

"Remember dear, you have to drive home."

When they had gone she still seemed to be distracted and annoyed. Joanne Greene leaned towards her.

"Let them go, they haven't seen each other for ages

133

and I've been dying to have a chat with you." She lifted a silver tray from the sideboard, loaded it with glasses and a bottle.

"If you can't beat them, join them, that's my motto," she said carrying the tray across the room. She sat down then leaned over and put her firm hand over Pamela's frail one.

"Having a child will make a difference, you know how much he has wanted one - it'll put that other nonsense out of his mind ..."

She stopped suddenly, quelled by the look in Pamela's eyes, put her hand over her mouth and looked at Kate.

Kate stared back at them, feeling gauche and inferior.

She could see hostility in their eyes.

I know all of *Lycidas*, she thought. I can scan it and parse it. You two probably think Milton is a disinfectant.

Had she spoken aloud? They seemed to be looking towards her strangely. She stared back at them panic-stricken. She began to sweat and blundered to her feet, knocking a small glass dog from the table.

"Do you mind if I go out to the garden?"

"Of course not, dear," said Joanne Greene jumping up too quickly and opening the French doors. "Go out and look around. The roses are in bloom, Alan looks after them, God knows how, I don't think they're a suitable plant for this windswept countryside."

Kate clumped across the room and out through the door in her big brown lace-up shoes.

"Sorry about my big mouth, I forgot we weren't alone. Who on earth is she?" Joanne asked quietly as Kate left.

"Oh, need you ask?" a tired voice replied. "Another one of Robert's lame ducks."

The door was politely but firmly closed behind her.

At last she was alone. She needed solitude, people flustered her. Had she changed so much in two years? It was late evening and she saw that the garden was wild and beautiful, a balm to her troubled mind. She wandered around for over an hour and then went back and peeped through the glass door. She could see Mrs Greene refilling two glasses, she could hear them laughing. They were obviously in excellent humour.

If I go back in now, they'll be reserved and polite. Their evening will be spoiled.

She went back and sat under a large chestnut tree. A wooden seat spanned its wide girth. The air was still, drenched with the smell of roses. To the West, where the sun was setting, she could see the distant ocean. It had been a long day and she was very tired. She closed her eyes.

She didn't know how long she slept, an hour, a minute, but when she woke the sun had set and there was a coldness in the air - Steele was standing a little distance away watching her.

"Well, had you a nice evening?" he said, walking over and smiling down at her.

"Lovely, thank you."

He sat down beside her, she turned around to speak to him but he held his finger to his lips, then leaning close to her pointed to a fuchsia hedge close beside them - suddenly a blackbird began to sing. From where they sat they could see the bird on a sturdy branch, feet firmly grasping, chest out, his yellow beak warbling the notes. Steele slid his arm around her shoulder, then drew her close. In silence they listened to the sweet pure sounds. In the fading light she turned her face to him and he kissed her gently.

From his breath came a mingling of alcohol and cigars, a pleasant male smell. Somewhere near a door banged - the bird stopped singing.

He sat back releasing her.

"I would be content to sit here forever with you, but..."

He pulled her to her feet and walked down the garden beside her holding her hand. Just before they came to the back door he squeezed it gently then dropped it. They walked casually into the house.

Alan Greene was standing at the kitchen sink. On the draining-board a huge salmon lay on a pile of newspapers.

"Christ no, you've done enough for us," Steele said when he realised that the fish was for them.

"Nonsense man," Greene was wrapping the paper tenderly around the fish. He brushed Steele's protests aside and carried it to the boot of the car. There he found an old fishing jacket and make it into a pillow for Kate. They made her lie down in the back of the car and covered her with a Foxford rug.

From where she lay in the back of the car she could hear a drift of voices.

"It was so nice a while ago," Pamela Steele was saying. "Look how dark the sky is now."

"Don't forget to let us know as soon as anything happens." She could see Joanne's hand checking the doors of the car.

"Heavens, it's not for ages, you'll be down to see us before then. Don't forget, you'll be godparents."

"Goodbye."

"Goodbye and God bless."

They slid into the night.

They travelled fast along empty roads. Kate lay somewhere between sleeping and waking. Occasionally she opened her eyes and looked out at the moon riding swiftly along with them, high up in the trees. From the front of the car she could hear the sound of voices: a married couple, happy together, returning home after a pleasant day visiting friends. Lying in the back of the car she was happy too. She could still feel the tranquillity that had flowed through her in the garden when Steele had held her in his arms. Once again she could feel his lips gentle on hers. She had never felt so close to another human being.

She was almost asleep when, a long time later, she felt the car climbing a steep hill. She knew that she was home. They roused her and she climbed sleepily out of the car and went over to the front door. She stood fumbling at the letterbox until she saw the car move away before she pulled the string in the door. She didn't want Pamela Steele to see her undignified mode of entry.

* * *

Harriet met her in the hall, her face pale and anxious.

"What in heaven's name kept you out until this time of the night ... do you not know that it's all hours ... what can that doctor be thinking about!"

"We were visiting a consultant in a chest hospital somewhere in Donegal. Some friend of the doctor, he wanted to discuss my case with him ... Mrs Steele came too," she added casually.

137

"What a relief." Her mother rubbed her forehead, looking confused. Her voice was hesitant as they walked into the kitchen.

"I suppose it's spending so much time alone, I get funny thoughts. Queer ideas come into my mind. I didn't know that Mrs Steele was going, she's such a nice woman, one of the Allens. I'm sure that she would know me..."

She stopped suddenly, remembering that people who once knew her were not interested in knowing her any more.

She sat drinking a cup of tea while Kate told her about the Greene's house.

"Every room had a cream carpet," she said, "not a square in the centre of the room with a margin of stain around the edge, but carpets that stretched out to the edge of the room."

Harriet nodded, "Wall to wall carpeting," she said. "It's the latest thing in America, I've seen it at the pictures."

"There was no pattern on it," Kate added.

"I know, although how they manage to lift it up to brush and beat it I don't understand."

"They clean it with a hoover," Kate told her.

"I saw them things in England," Harriet said, "demonstrations in the shops. They were just coming in when the War started. But they'll never be a success, they're just a flash in the pan. How could you suck the dirt out of a big heavy thing that you walk on all day? There's only one way to clean a carpet: wait for a Spring day, a good breezy day, throw it over the clothesline and beat it with a brush." Her hands flailed the air. "But you have to wear a turban because of the dust." She wove an imaginary turban around her head, carefully tucking the ends underneath.

"The bedrooms," Kate told her, "were all different colours. There was a pink one with silver hair brushes on the dressing-table."

"The master bedroom," Harriet nodded.

"The wardrobes were all fitted into the walls and lined with mirrors."

Harriet listened attentively.

"What kind of furniture did they have in the drawing room?"

Kate saw her eye slide hopefully towards her own pieces.

"It was white and shiny, a new type of wood. Even the hot coffee pot didn't mark it. It never needs polishing."

It was getting to her. Kate could see her shoulders droop, a frown of discontent appearing between her brows as she looked around the kitchen.

She stood up.

"I'll go up first," she said "come straight up."

She climbed the stairs heavily. Kate looked around with a sneer of contempt. Under the bannisters was the green velour chaise longue, its decorated mahogany swirling into infinity. In the centre of the room was the round mahogany table standing on a pod. Her mother polished it daily. At either side of the old stove were the brown leather armchairs, warm and deep, even the small table beside the window was solid mahogany. Nothing was bought with a thought of the house that they lived in, every piece was a memory of the past and a message of hope for the future. Yet Kate had deliberately destroyed her faith in what she had, let her know that styles were changing, people were moving on, while they remained here, fossilised.

She put out the light and climbed the stairs. There were none of the familiar sounds from Harriet's room as she passed by, the sighs and grunts as she undressed. There was only a silence - the silence of despair.

Kate knew her mother would have despised the furniture she had seen that day, just as she knew who - for all their posturings - was the real lady. Yet she had a strange feeling of satisfaction, of revenge, as she walked along the pale landing to her bedroom.

Chapter Four

Harriet came into Kate's bedroom waving an envelope.

"Wakey, wakey!" She was in good humour.

Kate sat up in surprise.

"A letter? Are you sure it's for me?"

"Well, your name's on it and it looks official, there's a crown on it."

She stood and looked out from behind the lace curtains feigning disinterest while Kate opened the envelope. A book fell out.

"It's like your pension book." She turned the strange book over.

"No," Harriet said coming over to peer at it. "It

must be the book for your disability payments. Do you remember me sending the form off last June?"

"So it is," Kate said, leafing through it. "Two pounds a week, and look - it's back-dated for eight weeks."

They stared at each other in disbelief. Until now Kate's pocket money had been a brass threepenny piece every Saturday. Now she would have money for clothes, for shoes, she could buy a lipstick, a new nightdress.

"Don't forget to thank the doctor for this," said Harriet "We'd never have known about it only for him."

Kate kept the envelope under her pillow. She thought that he would never come. Maybe he won't call today, she thought. But he did. As the Cathedral clock struck eleven he came through the door. Kate held the letter in front of her face.

"Snap!" he said, taking a letter from his inside pocket.

"Well, who goes first?"

"You do."

He sat opposite her on the bed. His eyes were shining.

"You've got a reprieve."

Her heart gave a flutter and began to thump heavily.

"Remember the blood tests I've been doing since last April? Well, I didn't tell you but your blood sedimentation rate has been falling steadily, now it's normal. You can get up for four hours a day."

"I can get up and just walk out? Go around on my own?" It seemed impossible after all this time.

He nodded smiling.

"We've arranged an x-ray for you at the end of the month but the lesion in your lung calcified a long time ago. I don't think it will present any problem."

She felt a wave of elation followed immediately by a feeling of depression. Something tickled her cheek. She brushed her face with the back of her hand - it was wet with tears. She began to cry. Steele pushed a large white handkerchief into her hand and walked to the window.

"I'm sorry." Now she was a hiccuping, sobbing mess.

"Don't worry, your emotions are a bit haywire. It's all very sudden. I sent the last blood sample in a few days ago. I suppose I should have told you that my little experiment seemed to be working but I wanted it to be a surprise."

He stood with his back to her gazing through the window giving her time to compose herself.

She had thought it would never happen. "Can I get up today?"

"There's no reason why you can't get up from two until six, so long as you stay around the house." He turned around, came over and sat on the edge of the bed. He reached out and took her hand.

"You can go out tomorrow, the day after and every day after that. By the way, does this house have a back garden?"

"No, just a yard."

He dropped her hand and stood up. There seemed to be nothing more to say.

"Well, I haven't started my calls yet." His voice was strained. "I'd better be off."

"Goodbye,"

"Goodbye."

She heard his car purr gently to the end of the street and just had time to crawl down the bed to the Catholic window to see it disappear around the corner. In the distance she could see Lowry figures climbing the steps of the Cathedral to attend morning mass. From tomorrow she would be back on the treadmill. She lay across the bed and began to sob. She could hear herself cry, gulp for air. She forgot about all the lonely days when she waited for the school friends who did not call, the mornings that she wakened at seven knowing she could do nothing but lie there until midnight when she would fall into a troubled sleep - she only thought of Steele and how much she would miss him. She wished that her blood sedimentation rate had gone higher and that her lungs had huge cavities. She wanted to see his agonised face bending over her bed while she sweated her life away. Once, when he had come up to her room and found her crying because she had spent a long day on her own, he had said with irritation, "You'll just have to stop feeling sorry for yourself, Kate, you are one of the lucky ones who will be cured of tuberculosis. I've just come from seeing a wee girl the same age as you who had to have every tooth in her head pulled out."

The horror of it. Eighteen years of age and no teeth. Nobody could be beautiful without their teeth. Imagine trying to eat. Yet she was still able to feel a stab of jealousy towards the unknown girl because Steele was so sorry for her and a sneaking feeling of satisfaction that she must now be mumbling and toothless and not very attractive. She didn't want anything like that to happen to her. She wanted to fade away like Mimi - beautiful and unforgettable.

By midday she had cheered up, after all she could still call to the surgery to see Steele - he had to monitor her condition. She still had many x-rays ahead of her. By two she was dressed and sitting in the brown leather armchair reading a book. The fire, too hot for the warm day, was making her sleepy. She still had a feeling of depression, of anti-climax. She walked over and leaned against the open door to the scullery. Her mother stood at the big stone sink peeling potatoes. Kate faced her back.

"Mum, I want to ask you something. Something important."

Come inside, she wanted to scream. Dry your hands on a towel as you always do when you come in from the kitchen. Sit down and listen to me. I must talk to somebody.

But Harriet didn't turn around, didn't answer although Kate had seen an almost imperceptible stiffening of her back.

"If you happen to fall in love with someone that you can't - mustn't fall in love with, what can you do about it?"

The words were torn from her like a sob. But her mother must understand. At eighteen she had run away with a papist, she, the daughter of the town's leading orangeman. There had to be suffering in her past. She thought that she saw a flush appear along the back of Harriet's neck. She was peeling an apple, a big misshapen bramley. The green parings broke and fell among the coarse potato peelings but they curled separately and did not mingle with them. She looked down at them and said nothing. In the silence Kate could hear the ticking of the clock, her own strained breathing.

Shaking, she returned to the chair. She could feel her face go red with shame. She thinks I was asking her about her past and I was only trying to tell her about myself.

What can I do? she thought. Where can I go for advice? With relief, she heard someone pull the string in the front door.

"Who in the name of Heavens could that be?" Harriet came in from the scullery, her hand balled tight against her chest. Visitors terrified her. Steele walked in. He smiled at Kate.

"Good, you're up and dressed, I have to see a patient in the country. You may as well come."

Kate stood up, her spirits rising. How glad she was to see him.

"I'll keep your dinner," her mother said, but Kate was closing the door as she spoke.

It was a relief to be out of the house and sitting in the car beside Steele again. She felt more relaxed with him than she did with her mother.

"I don't have to see a patient but I want to talk to you. I think the news this morning was something of a shock." He drove the car carefully, squinting against the sun. "You're moving into a new phase of your illness now, you are convalescing and it's important that you take good care of yourself and that you're free from any kind of anxiety."

"Where are we going?"

"To the mountains. There's nothing like the mountains for putting our troubles in perspective. When Jesus was troubled, He always went to the mountains. Do you remember that from your bible classes?"

"No. I'm a Catholic, we don't go in for bible reading

as much as you people."

* * *

The car was climbing higher and higher into the green hills.

"I didn't know we had places like this around us," Kate remarked.

"The Border runs along here, some of these fields are actually in the Irish Republic. It's beautiful, isn't it Kate? But all you have is scenery - it's damned hard to scratch a living here. Rocks and heather, the land is only fit to graze sheep and goats."

"You seem to know a lot about it."

"I grew up here. My father was a small farmer. I'm a country boy."

He smiled across at her, slowed down and parked the car.

"I'll show you what it's like - we're going for a walk." He leapt out of the car, walked around and opened the door for Kate. "The heather is blooming and it's very beautiful, you'll see."

They walked along springy turf under a lowering sky. On distant hills the two great churches brooded over the City.

"Two roads running parallel to God." she said.

"Yes, and only one wee man up there."

"But you must have a Catholic and a Protestant church."

From behind he put his hands gently on her shoulders. She flinched at his touch.

"I don't give a damn about those big churches. Do you see those little houses in the valley between?"

She looked at the layers of crooked-roofed houses,

147

postcard pretty in the distance.

"That's where my interest lies, where I spend most of my life. There I bring children into the world who will go through life without a shoe on their foot or an arse in their pants, there I see women who have grown old before their time - worn out with childbearing. These people are the salt of the earth, they deserve the best. Surely if there's any money available it should go towards healthcare for them or be invested in industry to give them a future ... but this is my hobby horse and it's not what I came out here to talk about."

He turned her round to face him. A tremor ran through her body and he let his hands fall to his sides. "Kate ..."

Just then a drop of rain hit her on the nose, then another and another. Steele grabbed her hand and they ran to the car. They reached it just in time. Rain spattered the roof as they hastily rolled up the windows.

"That was a sudden change," Kate gasped as she slid low in her seat and listened to the rain beat on the roof of the car.

"It's always like this up here. If you look down across the valley you can see the clouds swirling in from the distance long before the rain comes."

The rain grew heavier and the car was enveloped in clouds of mist.

They sat isolated, detached from the world.

This is where he is happiest, she thought. Nature is his God.

"Are you a pantheist?"

"Honestly pet, sometimes you're too deep for me. I'm a country GP - not a classical scholar..."

He sat tapping his fingers against the steering wheel and looking across at her.

"Do you remember the day I brought you to Donegal and you met Alan Greene?"

"Yes." Suddenly she was scared, she remembered Steele saying that he was going to discuss her case history with him. Like many chronically ill people she had become morbidly interested in the progress of her disease. He stared straight ahead of him through the windscreen. Then, as though he had made a decision he turned to her and said,

"He thinks you should attend another doctor."

She gulped. "Am I very ill?"

He looked uncomfortable.

"He thinks you've fallen in love with me."

Her mouth went dry, her heart began to thump.

"No," her voice was shaking, "that's not true."

She bent her head and put her face in her hands. He put his arms around her and drew her head onto his chest and gently stroked her hair.

"Kate, please don't be so upset. We're such close friends - I thought you could tell me anything."

She tried to slide from his arms but he held her tightly.

"Katie," he whispered "you are in love with me, aren't you?"

"Yes." She felt relief that she could tell someone. She waited for the laugh of derision but there was silence. With a tremendous effort she pulled herself away from him and hunched, weeping, over near the door of the car. Tears of rain ran down the windscreen of the car. Steele turned the wipers on, they whirred gently. Kate looked up and saw green spiky grass, washed stone. When he switched the wipers off there was a sudden silence, broken by a burst of hail drumming on the roof. Inside, the car was warm and muggy, curiously intimate. Now she longed for him to reach out and hold her but he made no move to touch her again.

"How did you know?"

He shrugged.

"I didn't take Greene too seriously, he doesn't always approve of my unorthodox ways of treating patients but he made me more aware of things, and I noticed the way you reacted if I touched you, even accidentally - as if you'd been shot."

"I'm sorry, I didn't mean it to happen."

"Believe me pet, I understand. It's like being hit across the head with a hammer when you least expect it."

That is exactly what it's like, she thought, he knew what he was talking about. Who had he loved to understand so well? Whoever it was, Kate hated her.

"And don't forget that at your age, you were bound to fall in love with somebody, your field of choice was very narrow."

"Now you'll tell me that every woman falls in love with her doctor."

"Well, don't they?" he was laughing but she felt a stab of jealousy towards all the women who may have loved him.

She sneaked a look towards him. He was staring towards the streaming windscreen, his eyes narrowed in thought. Soon he would turn around and tell her that he had come to a decision. With great reluctance he would have to transfer her to another GP, the rules which governed the conduct of a doctor towards his patients were very strict, where there was emotional involvement on either side he would have to walk away. Who would he hand her over to? There were only two other doctors in the town, Doctor McAdam, who Harriet attended, was an ancient, palsied man who should have retired years ago, and Doctor Murphy had recently developed a nervous blink in one eye which gave the questions he had to ask of his patients a new and often hilarious dimension.

"Who are you going to hand me over to?" she said at last.

He looked at her in surprise.

"Who says I'm going to hand you over to anyone?"

"I thought it was something to do with the Hippocratic oath - you can't get involved with a patient."

"I'm not involved."

He switched the engine on and they sat for a moment in the throbbing car.

"I'm safe." he said, "my friendship with you doesn't jar my conscience. I'm forty, sweetheart, or near enough to it, and married. I also have some personal honour and integrity you know. If I felt involved, I wouldn't be sitting here talking to you now. Anyway you're on the mend now, Kate, we'll be seeing less of each other."

He looked at her fondly.

"You'll have to get yourself a boyfriend, you must make normal healthy relationships with people your own age. Don't waste your affection on me, love, I'm not worth it."

He drove slowly home.

"You reminded Greene of someone, a girl I met when I worked in Dublin - she was a medical student in the Adelaide."

"Did you like her?"

He smiled to himself.

"You could say that. We were to be married."

"What happened?"

"Some bitch of a nurse told her I was two-timing her."

"And were you?"

"I was not!" He shouted with such vehemence that Kate jumped. Somehow the very force of his denial made her doubt its veracity.

"Did she break the romance off?"

"She qualified then went out to Africa for a year to work with the nuns to think things over. She was a Roman like yourself."

"Would you have become a Catholic to marry her?"

"I'd have become a Zulu warrior if that was what she wanted."

"And she decided not to marry you?"

The car went faster, the speedometer climbed. Kate felt frightened. She looked across at Steele, his upper lip was beaded with perspiration. But he had registered her look and immediately slowed down.

"When she was out there three months she contracted diphtheria. She hadn't a chance. A few years later the miracle drugs were on the market ... she could have been saved."

"And you blame yourself for what happened?"

He sighed.

"I went to pieces for a while ... drank too much. Alan Greene and Joanne held me together; later they introduced me to Pam."

They had reached her front door.

"I'll return the books you lent me," she said formally.

"There's no hurry, actually I brought you some *National Geographic* magazines." He pointed to the back seat of the car where they lay.

"Oh," she said, leaning over and picking them up and looking at their familiar yellow covers. "We used to have those magazines in the school library. The nuns used to glue together any pages they didn't want us to see."

"Like what?"

"Naked black people."

She thought he would be amused but when she looked over he was annoyed.

"Don't you think the world might be a better place if the religious had left the black people to their nakedness? I wonder what little nun was given the job of deciding which pages were offensive? Was sticking the pages together a punishment or a reward?"

Kate laughed.

"I must admit it was only the older nuns who had that attitude, the younger ones taught us the meaning of right and wrong and then left it to ourselves to make up our own minds. They believed in Free Will."

"Well at least you didn't get your education in the Irish Republic. There they have a strict form of censorship and an education system where children have to be taught Irish. Most of them have to emigrate to England or America - to their credit some of them are doing very well. Now take you, Kate. Did anyone ever teach you the facts of life, at school or at home?"

She shook her head.

"Do you understand why you have a period, or how a girl gets pregnant?"

"No."

He rubbed his eyes tiredly.

"Oh God, and you're a young woman now. Why do parents confuse ignorance and innocence? Would you like me to teach you?"

"Would you?"

"Of course pet, just start by reading these books. It should be an ongoing thing. The birds and the bees - you know. What will you do with your time tomorrow?"

She shrugged.

"Hang around the house, I suppose."

"Do you know how to get around to the back garden of my house?"

She shook her head.

"Go down the entry before you come to the house. It's the second door, the black one. Come down tomorrow afternoon."

She got out of the car uneasily, knowing he had invited her down to his garden on an impulse, it was not something he had planned. She peeped in at him before she shut the door.

"About tomorrow, are you sure?"

"Of course I am." He looked over at the house. "I couldn't bear to think of you sitting in that mausoleum all day. Now off you go - and don't forget your books."

Chapter Five

"Will you come down the town with me?"

She waved her payment book at her mother to lure her.

"You're not carrying that thing in your hand for every Tom, Dick and Harry to know your business."

Harriet went into the cupboard under the stairs and came out with an ancient leather handbag.

"I'm not carrying that thing. It reaches down to my knees."

"You'll do as you're told, Miss."

She put the book into the huge empty bag and closed its ancient brass fastener. The edges of the flap were mouldy green. They curled pathetically towards her.

"Will you come? I want to buy clothes - you could help me."

Harriet looked around the spotless room. "I've to do some cleaning."

"You've nothing to do, the room is lovely. Come on, please?"

She walked towards her and held her hand out.

But her mother backed away.

"The bedroom upstairs needs to be swept."

Kate went towards the door and stopped with her heart thumping.

"Everyone will look at me."

"Don't be silly, they'll not give you a second thought."

"I might get weak."

"No, you'll not, you're as strong as a horse."

She sat down again, playing for time. "Where will I get the clothes?"

"Oh, go to Lomans, they're expensive but they have good stuff."

"Ciara's mother won't go there to shop. She says they're oul' black prods who don't employ Catholics."

Harriet stiffened and her face grew red.

"They are not black. I don't see many Catholic shops employing Protestants, but more to the point their clothes are good. Go on," she laughed, "the shops will be closed by the time you get out of the house."

Kate went to the front door. Her head grew dizzy but she took a deep breath and stepped onto the footpath. She longed for Steele's car to be there so that she could jump into it. She walked along the curving semicircle of houses close to the wall. Her knuckles tore on the old stone. Old Mr McAfee stood gasping at his front door. His face was yellow with age and asthma.

"Hello," she said. She had never spoken to him before. His eyes rounded with surprise.

"Hello," he wheezed.

She heard him turn slowly around and shuffle down the hall to tell everyone in the family that she was up and about. When at last she reached the main street she mingled thankfully with the crowd. Familiar faces loomed in front of her. Catholic and Protestant faces. She had grown up in this town and she knew that there were Catholic and Protestant shops, streets where mostly Protestants shopped and others patronised by Catholics. Only on the main street did they shop side by side, in uneasy fraternity. But although Kate knew this, the division would not have been obvious to a stranger. The little market town had a veneer of normality. The sun was shining brightly, gay canopies hung down over shop-fronts. Everyone was wearing bright Summer clothes. She felt shabby and odd in the jigger and the heavy grey skirt. She went into the Post Office and presented her payment book to the clerk behind the counter. He opened the book and leafed through it, then looked at her. She stood poised, trembling, ready to run.

You're not entitled to this money, he would say loudly, pointing an accusing finger at her. Stop thief, he would shout as she ran for the door.

But without another glance at her he stamped the pages of the book, tore out the thin sheets and counted the stiff new notes onto the counter.

"Here you are, dear," he said pushing them towards her.

She dropped the notes into the bottom of the big leather bag and came back up the town. She felt that she was veering from one side of the footpath to the other.

Don't panic, she thought. Forget about yourself. Nobody knows you. They don't realise that you haven't been out on your own for over two years. People aren't thinking about you. She remembered Steele telling her to hold her head up when she walked through the city. She relaxed, held her head high as she walked through the town. She went into Lomans shop and straight through the luxurious bottom floor, then she turned and walked up the thick-carpeted stairs to the dress department, where she bought two dresses and a cream silk shirt.

"I'll keep this dress on," she said to the shop assistant as she admired her outline in the mirror.

"That's alright, I'll put your own clothes in a bag. You'll easily manage them and your new ones," the assistant said.

She folded the heavy grey skirt and the jigger carefully and put them into an elegant bag while Kate looked at herself in the long narrow mirror. She couldn't believe the change that had taken place in her appearance in such a short time. The long walks with Steele and her increased attention to her diet had paid off and she now had the slim modern look she had so envied in the girls she'd seen walking along the street. But as she turned this way and that she could see her hair was lank and long and completely out of fashion.

"One half of you laughing at the other," she could hear her mother's voice.

She came out of the shop and crossed the road to

the hairdresser.

"A cut wash and set, please."

"Curls or waves, Miss?" the hairdresser asked when her hair had been washed and she was sitting down in front of a mirror, a damp towel around her neck.

"Waves."

Kate knew the same question was asked of all the customers and, no matter which answer they gave, they all came out with the same hairstyle. Ethel Lindsay only knew one style, a mixture of waves and curls cemented to the head with thick green setting lotion. Now she lifted a strand of Kate's hair and narrowed her eyes behind thick spectacles. Just as she lifted her scissors to cut a young assistant came over,

"You're wanted on the telephone, Mrs Lindsay," she whispered.

Ethel frowned and looked around the crowded salon.

"Will you look after this head?" she said. "Otherwise we'll fall behind."

She waddled over to the telephone in the corner. The girl leaned over and spoke to Kate in the mirror.

"Hello, what way would you like your hair done? Curls or waves?"

They began to laugh.

"I'll leave it up to you," Kate said.

"If you leave it up to me I'd restyle it completely." She combed Kate's hair back from her face. "You have a lovely bone structure and beautiful skin, you should wear your hair very short and show it off. Shall I start?"

"Go ahead, I'll trust myself to you."

The girl went off and got a razor and began to cut Kate's hair.

"I'll leave it longer at the back and shape it into a duck's tail. They wear it like that in London now."

"Do you live in London?"

"Yea, I work with Sassoon. Mrs Lindsay's my aunt, I'm here visiting her and I'm giving her a hand at the moment. She won't let me near the customers, says that my way-out ideas will frighten them away."

As she talked she drew the razor expertly through Kate's hair.

"Were you young when you went to London?"

"Eighteen. I lived in the country and it wasn't for me. I had nothing to look forward to only working in this one-horse town. I bailed out and I've never regretted it."

"Were you lonely - at first, I mean?"

"No, my sister had already gone. I went over to her. You should go yourself, it changes you, broadens your mind."

As she talked, she cut Kate's hair as short as a boy's. As soon as it was finished, she took the towel from around her neck and carefully brushed the hair from her shoulders.

"Now," she said, "If you lived in London you couldn't have a more modern look. It's the very latest style."

Kate looked in the mirror and stared at herself in disbelief. Her face had taken on a different shape. The roundness of puberty had changed to the interesting hollows and shadows she had admired so often in the faces of actresses in the forbidden film books under the mattress.

She gave the amazed hairdresser a huge tip and came shyly out of the shop. A group of adolescent boys from the local Christian Brothers school lounged across their bicycles at the side of the road and chatted. They straightened up and looked at her. She plunged gratefully into the dark shoe shop beside Woolworths, and came out wearing a pair of red leather sandals. They squeaked pleasantly as she walked along. Then she went around to the fish and chip shop and bought two bags of fish and chips. The Italian behind the counter threw an extra scoop into the bag and winked at her. He squeezed her hand as he pressed the change into it. Feeling rather pleased with herself, she climbed the steep hill home. She put her head around the door where her mother was polishing the big centre table.

"Who's that?" she peered towards her in the gloomy room.

Kate walked closer.

Harriet stared at her, open-mouthed. Something cold and venomous snaked through her eyes momentarily.

Kate backed away.

"It's me."

Her mother's own sweet smile returned.

"Oh, you look lovely. For a moment I thought - you reminded me ..."

"Who did I remind you of?"

"Oh, nobody." Her eyes were veiled, wary. But who had she seen when she looked at her daughter?

Kate's dead father?

Her sisters who passed her in the main street with glacial eyes?

Herself, long ago?

Kate knew that she would never say.

* * *

An hour later she started down the hill with a breeze drifting around her bare legs and tugging the hem of her pale blue dress.

"Now Cinderella," said her mother as Kate was leaving. "You have to be home by six."

She reached the bottom of the hill and bumped into two girls as they came around the corner.

"Excuse me." They circled each other trying to pass.

"It's Kate!" one of them exclaimed. "Don't you know us?"

It was Ciara and her new friend, Mary Trimble. Ciara's visits to Kate had dropped off since Christmas Now they stopped beside her and a look of guilt spread over Ciara's face.

"We were just going to visit you."

Kate noticed Mary's gape of surprise and Ciara's quick nudge. They stood, embarrassed, a gulf of time between them. Three boys sidled along the footpath and stopped beside them. Mary began to giggle, Ciara looked at her with scorn and quirked a sardonic eyebrow towards Kate.

This fool, she was saying, she only became my friend because you weren't around.

The boys jostled each other towards them. Ciara introduced Kate. They were boarders at the local college, allowed out for the evening because their final examinations had just finished. In a few days, they would be leaving the school for good. Today one of them had done his 'A' levels in history as had Ciara. Now she stood, a little apart from Kate and Mary, talking to him and comparing notes. The other boy stood beside Kate and Mary, smiling towards them. Mary, who had very blonde hair and fair skin, was red with embarrassment. She stared towards the ground and said nothing.

"Where do you come from?" Kate asked him. She didn't really care where he came from but felt she had to say something to keep the flagging conversation going.

"I'm from the country," he said. "We farm up near the Border."

Her heart gave a lurch.

"I'm sorry, I didn't hear your name." she said, hoping and dreading that he might say Steele, then she remembered that he was a Catholic and Steele a Protestant and they couldn't be related. Apart from that, Steele would have been leaving for College when he was born. She looked at him, despising his youth.

"Raymond Callaghan,"

"I have to go."

As Kate walked away he pulled Mary by the arm. Kate walked on. Mary ran after her and jerked her head back toward him, Kate saw that she was close to tears.

"Ray says will you go to the flicks with him on Saturday?"

She had opened her mouth to say "no" when she remembered Steele's words, get yourself a boyfriend.

"Yes, I'll go."

"He says he'll meet you outside the Carlton at three."

Her first date.

Once she would have been thrilled. Now it meant nothing to her. A date with a callow youth, she thought. Most of the books she read had a callow youth in them somewhere. She turned and walked down the street to the houses where Steele lived. Her heart beat with excitement as she turned into the entry that serviced his block of houses. She had a strange guilty feeling that thrilled her.

My Secret Garden, she thought as she opened the latch of the black door leading to the back of his house. The garden was a lake of sunlight, bounded by high stone walls. It was dotted with shrubs, edged with flower beds. At the far end, an elderly man was digging the vegetable patch with a spade. He was wearing an ancient straw hat with a wide ragged brim. His shapeless vest hung out over his trousers which were shiny and loose in the seat. The trouser legs had been cut off jaggedly above the knee. Of Steele there was no sign. As she walked towards the old man she could see the white hairy legs and the battered shoes laced with string. In the quiet afternoon she could hear him hum contentedly as he worked. A toothless mumble, she thought.

"Excuse me...."

He turned and Kate caught a glimpse of his face. Steele. The flame of young romantic love flickered and almost died. He turned around completely, unabashed at her seeing him in his strange attire. He was smiling and looked pleased to see her.

"I wasn't sure if you'd come."

He leaned on the handle of the spade with one hand, raised his bare knee and pointed his toe like a ballet dancer.

"Isn't that a fine leg?"

They both laughed and the tension evaporated. Then he began to stare at her. He dug the spade into the ground and came towards her. He held his two hands out and took hers.

"Kate, you look beautiful. I knew that you were a pretty girl but this is really a transformation."

"The clothes make me look slimmer. And I have lost some weight too. Do you like my new hairstyle?"

"Yes, I like it, it makes you look very attractive. Too attractive." He stared at her silently until she hung her head shyly, then he said, "I'm sorry Pet, I didn't mean to stare. Come on, I'll show you my garden."

They walked Indian file along the narrow dirt paths which banded and crisscrossed the garden. She trotted obediently behind him, admiring his vegetables, his flowers, his trees. He was an excellent gardener, his vegetables were green and healthy, his flowers strong and colourful.

"Can I help you with weeding or anything?"

"You're not strong enough yet. Sit over there." He pointed to a rug on the grass. "Pamela was down earlier."

She sat on the rug and skimmed through the magazine which lay on the rug. The sun burned through her light dress. She could feel the heat on her breast, her thighs. Every second she was aware that Steele was close beside her. Once again she felt, as she always did when she was with him, a peace stealing over her, a lessening of the anxiety that kept her constantly on the verge of tears - she always had a feeling of rightness in being with him.

If I had always known him, she thought, I would never have become ill, and she understood why he had treated her disease as a sickness of the spirit as much as of the body. I want to be with him always, she thought, I could never survive without his strength. She was looking over at him and he looked up from his work suddenly and caught her unguarded face. They stared towards each other. He dropped his eyes first. For the first time ever he seemed to be shy, ill at ease.

"Your farming background shows," she said to hide her embarrassment.

"Come on, it's time to water my tomato plants." He plunged his spade upright into the soil and walked towards her. He put his hand out and pulled her to her feet.

"Some men have their etchings, some have their tomato plants."

She stood inside the door of the greenhouse and watched him spray the tall plants. The air was heavy, humid and filled with the smell of soil - wet and leafy. Tomatoes, red and obscene, hung fat and ripe from the plants.

I can almost smell things growing here, Kate thought. She felt nauseated, her skin was damp, clammy. She stumbled. Steele was beside her instantly.

"You don't like it in here."

His hand quickly, professionally felt her brow.

"It's too ... rich."

"Do you feel faint?"

She nodded, unable to speak. He steered her outside and sat her gently down on a rustic bench fitted into a stone alcove. He sat beside her.

"You'll soon recover in the fresh air."

He pushed her reeling head between her knees. Gradually she began to feel better. She sat up slowly.

"You're the colour of death."

"Maybe I've caught TB again."

At the thought her heart began to thump, she began to whimper with panic.

"No, no, you haven't."

He put his arm around her shoulder and drew her close to his chest. He stroked her short hair, rocking her gently.

"Hush, don't be afraid, you're not sick again and you're not going to be. So don't be so anxious, just relax and let me look after your health."

Nobody had touched her with affection, reached out to her since her father died. She had felt that she was ugly and repulsive to people. Now she could feel the warmth of Steele's arm around her. She felt safe and happy.

Suddenly there was a loud screeching sound which brought Kate quickly to her feet. The wicket gate which led from the garden to Steele's house had been wrenched open. Lizzie Trodden was standing in the garden. Kate's head began to reel again. She felt strangely disorientated. This woman belonged only to King Street, to the Protestant window backed by the old Cathedral, to the dark side of Kate's life - not to here. Steele stood up and walked towards her while Kate stood staring. After throwing a look of blazing hatred in Kate's direction Lizzie avoided looking at her and talked only to Steele, but Kate could feel the woman's awareness of her and the tentacles of her hatred reaching towards her.

"Yes?"

Steele's voice was cold, tinged with annoyance, a doctor in his surgery being disturbed while with a patient.

"Mrs Steele sent me down for the cabbages, Doctor. She's been waiting for them."

"Oh, yes."

He pointed to where two cabbages were uprooted

and cleaned, lying on the vegetable patch. When she had left, Steele looked towards Kate.

"Great worker that woman but somehow I can't warm to her."

So she worked in his house.

"Why not?"

"I don't know but she has a fanatical look in her eye that I don't trust."

He came over and threw himself on the grass in front of her. He lifted a stem of grass and wove it through his fingers. He kept his head turned away from her.

"When she came in here just now I had my arms around you. Last week it wouldn't have mattered, today I felt guilty..."

He stood up and looked down at his hairy legs.

"What a silly old fool I am, talking like that. I'll go up and change."

"I'll go on home."

"Hang on, I'll drive you home. You still look a bit green around the gills."

He left through the wicket gate. She sat quietly on the warm sunny bench until he came back. She looked up at him and from where she sat she could see his broad straight shoulders under the soft material of his jacket. He stared down at her with hooded eyes, his expression inscrutable.

"Come on."

He glanced towards her as he drove.

"You'll have to get that boyfriend soon and let him escort you through the town. People will say that I'm a dirty old man."

"I've a date for the pictures on Saturday."

"With whom?" He looked surprised.

"A boy from the College. We've been writing to each other for two years," she lied, not wanting him to know that he had practically picked her up on the street.

"He goes to the College here in town? That place is a seminary, don't most of the pupils eventually become priests?"

"Raymond's going to become a doctor."

"What sort of doctor? A GP like me?"

She thought she caught a glint of amusement in his eyes.

"No, he's going to specialise in ... geriatrics." It was the only medical sounding term that she could think of.

"Geriatrics, how exciting. He's going to Queens?"

"No, he's going to Trinity College in Dublin." It had a cosmopolitan ring about it.

"He must be very dedicated to medicine when he is prepared to sacrifice his immortal soul for it."

"What do you mean?"

"Do you not know that Roman Catholics are excommunicated if they go to Trinity? They might be contaminated by outside ideas."

"Oh, but he's so clever, he got a dispensation."

He slowed his car to a halt. She was home again. He leaned across her and opened the car door to let her out.

"I can't stand clever people myself," he said. "They're usually one great big pain in the ass."

* * *

She came down the hill towards the cinema. She had no idea what her date looked like. Tall and dark?

Small and fair? No, she thought that he was taller than his two friends and that his hair was black. Even so, she had spent most of the morning standing at the mirror in her bedroom staring at her white face. Harriet came in to rub the window and tidy the curtains.

"You'll crack that mirror if you look in it much longer."

When she was sure that her mother had left the room she took a Pond's lipstick, which she had bought in Woolworths, from the top drawer and drew the magazines from under the mattress. She thumbed quickly to the double centre page which said: *Discover the hidden you.*

The page showed six different shapes of faces. She spread the magazine out on the bed and checked the shape of each face to see which was nearest to her own. They all looked much the same except two, one had a huge misshapen jaw, the other a bulbous forehead. She peered at each drawing and checked each one against the face that stared anxiously at her in the mirror.

"Oval," she breathed.

Underneath the picture the caption read: *Using a soft camel brush and powdered rouge, blend upwards and outwards with a soft flowing movement along the cheekbone.*

She rubbed lipstick into the palm of her hand and traced it along the lines of her cheekbones, trying to follow the shaded area of the oval face in the magazine. Her breath fogged the mirror. She heard her mother's step on the stairs and slid the magazine under the mattress.

She ran quickly out of the room and bumped into

her mother on the landing.

Harriet stopped and stared into her face.

"Are you feeling alright?"

"Yes, I feel great."

"You look a bit feverish."

"No, I'm alright. I'm going out for a wee while."

"Where to?"

She shrugged.

"I'll call for Ciara."

He was the only person outside the picture house, leaning against the wall in a bright green suit. When he saw Kate he straightened and walked towards her, smiling. He's not bad looking, she thought, trying to ignore his clothes. He had obviously dressed for the occasion, The day was hot and he was wearing a stiff starched collar which had left a red weal on his neck. His suit looked new but the material was hard and hairy and crisscrossed with a dazzling green check. He doesn't shop in Lomans, she thought, feeling svelte and sophisticated beside him. She averted her eyes from the row of fountain pens in his breast pocket and cringed at the army of badges which marched across the lapel of his jacket. He had a lot to learn. She thought with longing of Steele in his battered elegant tweeds. He escorted her into the cinema and over to the ticket box.

"Two one and nines," he said, taking a ten shilling note out of his wallet and throwing it onto the ticket desk. Kate was impressed. He obviously had money and didn't mind spending it. They were going to sit in the balcony. The foyer of the picture house was dim and luxurious, they walked towards the balcony stairs treading on thick carpet and seeing themselves reflected in a dozen mirrors. The usherette shone a torch and they stumbled down the balcony steps in the dim light.

"Here."

"Not down there, up this way."

Raymond was pushing her back up a few steps and into a row of seats. They were sitting near the back of the cinema. When they pulled the red plush seats down to sit in them they sprang back again. They began to laugh.

"Shhhh." The usherette waved a torch towards them. They sat down to watch the film. It was more than two years since Kate had been to a film and even then it had been a rare treat.

"It's for state days and bonfire nights," Harriet would say.

Kate loved the cinema, the colour, the clothes and most of all the fantastic stories. Harriet was also very fond of the pictures but never had anyone to go with. Occasionally she went by herself while Kate stayed at home.

"You can mind the house," Harriet would say.

When she came home she would tell her every detail of the film, walking around the big room acting out the parts while Kate drank in every word and gesture she made. Now Kate sat watching a film while her mother stayed at home and minded the house. But she would never be able to tell her mother the story. Unless, she thought, she said that she had gone with Ciara. She wouldn't mind that and Kate could tell her the story tonight.

"Who is the man?" Raymond asked.

"Glenn Ford," she whispered.

She thought he looked like Steele and she was following every move he made.

"Isn't the girl gorgeous?"

"The girl?" Kate had barely noticed her. "That's Rita Hayworth."

She was proud of her sophistication and amused by Raymond's gaucheness.

"The film is called *Gilda*," she whispered. "It's supposed to be great."

She was totally engrossed when a hand reached over and took hers. It was a soft, fleshy limb which clasped hers in an alien grip. She could hear Raymond breathing beside her.

An arm slid furtively around her shoulder and a face pressed close to hers, sweaty in the dark picture house and she wondered if he had pimples. She could hear her loud gulp of embarrassment. She sat and tried to concentrate on the film. But the magic had gone. Her neck was hurting where his arm lay between the back of her neck and the seat. She turned around to make herself more comfortable and a mouth was pressed hard on hers. She tried to protest and a tongue was pushed to the back of her throat. She almost gagged as she beat against his shoulders.

He sat back in his seat.

She sat staring at the screen, feeling sick. She thought she could feel a globule of foreign saliva in her mouth. She wished she had the courage to get up and walk out but she had not. She didn't want to appear uncouth, cause a scene. She couldn't even remember what Raymond looked like. The outline of his head appeared between her and the screen as he lunged again. This time she managed to clench her teeth like a vice and his probing tongue hit solid enamel. Undeterred, he began to kiss her eyes, behind her ears, his mouth moved to her neck. Suddenly he pushed her away roughly.

"What are you playing at?" he whispered in the darkness.

"What do you mean?"

"If you didn't want to come out for a coort you should have said so."

"I thought I was invited to the pictures," she said indignantly.

He lunged again. Kate didn't want to appear cold or unnatural, so she opened her mouth. But this time he just kissed her gently. She relaxed, this wasn't so bad after all, it was almost enjoyable. His hand slid over her shoulder, down her back, and he pulled at the fastening of her bra. She fought to get herself away from him and sat back aghast. He leaned towards her again.

"If you don't like me, why don't you say so?"

"It's not that, I just don't..."

"You don't want me to touch you."

"I don't know you."

"I can get plenty of girls, there's a girl working in the College, she could have anyone, she picked me."

Picked him for what, Kate wondered?

His head loomed large in front of her, blacking out the screen. His hot breath fanned her face. What am I doing here? she wondered. Why am I letting a total stranger paw all over me? Suddenly, she stood up and the seat snapped loudly into an upright position.

"Where are you going?"

"I'm leaving. You can stay here."

A sea of white luminous faces bobbed at her from the darkness as she trampled over feet.

"Excuse me, excuse me," she could hear Raymond behind her.

She climbed up the stairs to the back of the balcony and down the red carpeted staircase into the street. A dozen fleeing figures ran towards her from a myriad of mirrors.

"Kate, I'm sorry, wait please..." she could hear Raymond's voice.

She stopped and he caught up with her, they stood blinking at each other, two embarrassed strangers.

"Why did you do that? The film's only half over."

"I didn't even see that half." She turned and walked away. Raymond ran after her.

"Look, I've said I'm sorry about what happened in there."

They stood facing each other. Raymond kicked a small stone from one foot to the other. They both watched his feet. Then he looked over at her, his eyes brimming with laughter.

"Sure it was no great harm. It was only a wee coort - a bit of crack. I thought that's what girls wanted."

"Girls like to be treated with respect."

Her voice was brittle, authoritative, a school-marm's voice. The smile faded from his face, he stood looking miserable in the stiff green suit. Something like a spot of blood glistened on the red weal of his neck - he looked young and pathetic.

"Will you come down to Cafollas for a cup of coffee? I don't have to be back until six."

"No, thank you."

She turned to walk up the steep hill to King Street and suddenly she thought of the long evening sitting with her mother in the gloomy room.

She knew she could not bear it.

She turned and walked beside him down to Cafollas.

175

They sat and stared into their cups of frothy white coffee. Kate had taken a sip of hers and it was scalding; now she was breathing in through her mouth trying to cool her tongue.

"Look, I'm sorry about the flicks."

"It's OK." She thought for a moment, "I suppose you have to make hay while the sun shines."

He stared at her.

"What's that supposed to mean?"

"If you're going to be a priest ..."

"Somebody said that to you. Who told you that?"

"Mary told me."

He looked away from her then bent his head and turned the thick white cup around and around on the saucer.

"I can't explain," he looked up at her and she saw that he had deep blue eyes, gentle and thick-lashed. Any girl would be proud of those eyes, she thought.

"I don't want to be a priest. The loneliness, the total obedience ..." Suddenly he shivered. "Somebody walked over my grave. Anyway, I would like to have a profession, get married, have children ..."

"But why can't you do those things?"

"I don't know, I just know that I never will. Don't laugh but I have this feeling that God has called me ..."

"Maybe the priests in the College are trying to influence you to join them - it is a seminary," she said remembering what Steele had told her.

But Raymond was frowning.

"Who said that to you? That's Protestant Dick talking. Do you think that the priests would be so foolish? No, the call must come from within - or as they would say, from above."

He looked at her shyly.

"There's a poem called *The Hound Of Heaven* which explains it. *I fled Him down the nights and down the days ...*"

Kate nodded. "*All things betray thee, who betrayest Me ...*"

His mouth dropped open in surprise.

"I never met a girl who could quote poetry."

"Girls have minds too, you know. Besides I've had plenty of time to read poetry."

She told him about her years in bed.

"I'm not positive," she said, in case he would worry about having kissed her.

He laughed.

"I'm not worried, they'd hardly let you run around with some rampant infection. I'm surprised though, you have lovely rosy cheeks, you don't look like somebody who's been seriously ill ..."

Kate was glad she had decided to come down to the café with Raymond. They sat chatting easily, and Kate found it was pleasant to be with somebody her own age. In the booths up and down the shop, girls and boys were sitting together listening to music from the jukebox.

"Kate," he leaned towards her finally. "I just want to say how much I have enjoyed this afternoon. I have never told anyone the things that I told you today. I hate to leave but I have to go now, we have tea at six."

Outside the shop he said to her, "Would you meet me next week? We finish up on Monday and I'll be going home for the Summer. I'll have to help around the farm during the week but I could meet you next Saturday ..."

It would be nice to meet him she thought, after a

bad start they had got on very well. He was very handsome, not a pimple in sight, she had checked that out as soon as they sat opposite each other in the café. They were standing at the edge of the footpath on the main street where the road narrowed to a bottle-neck. There was a constant build-up of traffic. With a racing heart she saw Steele's car slow down in the line of traffic, she was so near to it that she could have touched the bonnet. She raised her hand to wave and saw that he was not alone, that somebody sat beside him in the front seat. At first she thought it was his wife, then she saw it was a girl in her early twenties. Kate had an impression of blonde hair and a blouse that was silky white. As she looked, she saw the girl lean towards him with an easy familiarity - saw her stretch her hand to his shoulder and talk eagerly to him, saw his face beam with pleasure as he revved up the car and drove off.

"Well, is it a date?"

She turned back to Raymond with a sneer.

"Why do you wear those awful badges in your lapel? And you have at least four pens in your pocket. As for your suit, it's the colour of senna."

He looked at her, speechless with shock. Time stood still as she watched his mouth open and close like a fish. She was fascinated to see his Adam's apple move up and down.

"The whole outfit is not in very good taste."

She could hear her mother's voice bitter and wounding.

He was still gulping for air when she turned and ran.

* * *

She could hear herself sobbing as she ran up the almost perpendicular hill. She stopped to catch her breath at an almost-level place where she had always stopped as a child. Her chest was wracked with pain. From the Cathedral high on the hill in front of her came the deep male sound of an organ - then, as it died away, the air was filled with the sweet sound of a soprano boys' choir. She had often heard this singing from her sick bed, the church choir practised on Saturday evenings for Sunday matins - as always the clear pure tones ringing over the still air affected her deeply. She continued slowly up to the top of the hill listening to the music. She walked quietly through King Street but when she pulled the string in her front door the tears came.

"In the name of Heavens, what's wrong?" Harriet straightened up from the stove with a tea-towel in her hand. Her face was flushed, there was a streak of flour in her dark hair - obviously she had been baking all afternoon. At the cool end of the stove there were apple tarts. Beside them was a golden pie in a blue enamel dish, behind them a mountain of pancakes. She stood shyly displaying her wares.

"Well, I hope you have a good appetite." She was looking at Kate with concern.

"I'm not hungry."

"Who's going to eat all this?" It was a cry of alarm.

"I don't know and I don't care. Eat them yourself."

She ran past her mother up to the safety of her room. She threw herself across the bed and sobbed her heart out. Some part of her stood aside and cynically watched the display of grief, the deep wracking sobs, the kicking feet, the saliva-covered hands and face. At last the calm came when she could cry no more, the shaking stopped and she lay on the bed, emotionally drained. After a while, beginning to feel cold and stiff, she crept over to the mirror and examined her face with interest. Her bloodshot eyes had sunk behind red rims, her face was puffy and mottled. The hand that reached to her swollen lips was trembling. She looked at herself with strange satisfaction. Look what love has done to me, she thought. I will never survive, She undressed and climbed into bed.

She curled up in a ball of misery and fell asleep.

Steele drove past her again. Now he was not Steele but Glenn Ford. Beside him sat Rita Hayworth and as she passed Kate she threw her a look of triumph and put her hand on his shoulder in a familiar, provocative gesture. Now he was kissing her, kissing her eyes and her mouth, but now she was Kate and Glenn Ford was Steele again and she was lying back in his arms and slowly opening her mouth to his probing tongue.

She was wrenched into wakefulness by a loud knocking on her bedroom door. Her dream was fading and she lay there with a memory of guilty pleasure. Then she remembered the dream in full and was filled with panic. How had she dreamed these things of Steele, a married man? The handle of the bedroom door turned, the door was pushed open, Ciara poked her head in.

"May we come in?"

She came into the room with a smile. Mary Trimble tiptoed behind her, lifting her knees high like she was attempting a weird tribal dance. They sat one on each side of the bed and stared at her.

"Your mother said that we could come up and visit you."

"She gave us tea and apple tart, it was gorgeous."

They continued to stare at her until she began to shift uncomfortably.

"Well?"

"Well what?"

"Your date, how did it go?"

"I saw him going to meet you, God he looked gorgeous. The back seat I suppose?"

She gave Kate a slow sly wink.

Kate was almost certain that Mary had never been out on a date with a boy but she had three older sisters and by listening to them she had become an expert on the behaviour of courting couples. Before she could answer, Ciara pulled a green woodbine packet from her pocket and passed it around.

"My mother gave me money to buy you oranges but I knew you'd prefer these."

Kate looked at the proffered cigarettes nervously.

"Do you think I should smoke? I mean my lungs."

"Who'll know? Do you remember before you got sick how we used to go out to the graveyard and smoke?"

Was it only two years ago that they sat behind the headstones and puffed furtively? These girls had changed so little, they sounded young and silly. They lit the cigarettes and she leaned back on the pillows.

"Did he French kiss you?"

Mary leaned towards Kate with avid curiosity.

"Oh sure, it was great," she said, pushing the horror of it to the back of her mind and flicking ash all over the white counterpane. Ciara reached over, lifted a saucer from the dressing-table and handed it to Kate.

"French kissing is a mortal sin." she said.

Kate's heart thumped with fright. A mortal sin. But she had no feeling of guilt - that struggle in the back of the cinema could not have been sinful. She had done everything to resist his unwanted embraces. Then she thought of Steele and her dream and was flooded with embarrassment. Ciara saw the sudden rush of blood to her face.

"When you go to Confession you should go to Father McGlinchey," she said looking at Kate with sympathy. "Our Eileen says he'd let you off with anything. He doesn't listen half the time. And if you have a problem you can talk to him."

Kate picked at a thin silk thread which formed a motif on the bedspread. She rolled it into a small sticky ball in her hand and watched the embroidered daisies disappear from the bedspread like falling dominoes. Maybe she could go to Father McGlinchey and tell him of her feelings about Steele. She pictured him leaning towards her in the confession box, counselling her, giving her advice.

She was tired now and wished they would leave. But they had passed the cigarettes around again, Ciara puffed contentedly as she lay sprawled across the bottom of the bed, Mary had her knees drawn up into the old armchair that she had pulled up beside the bed.

"Did Raymond say that he knows me very well?"

Kate looked at Mary and was about to shake her head when she realised that Mary was in love with him. She could see her hands were trembling, and suddenly realised the effort that it cost her to ask the question. She pushed the saucer quickly under the falling ash. If only I had known I would never have gone out with him, she thought.

"He said that you were very nice and that you have beautiful hair."

It was a lie but it was worth it, she thought when she saw Mary's plain face suddenly suffused with radiance.

"If you see him again will you tell him I was asking for him?"

"She's cracked about him," said Ciara, nodding at Mary.

Mary looked at her, stunned at her treachery.

"I am not, he's going to be a priest."

"It's always the same," said Ciara. "The smashers always go."

They finished the cigarettes and put the butts into the saucer. Ciara handed the packet around again.

"The exams are finished at last, thank God." she said, lying across the bed and staring at the ceiling. "I've failed, of course."

They all knew that Ciara would do well and go to University with her sister.

"Is Raymond worried about his results?" Mary asked. She was obsessed with him. Kate wondered if that was how she sounded about Steele.

"You seem to go out a lot with Dr Steele in his car," said Ciara. She, too, was a patient of Steele. "I saw him with a dame in his car today, she was a real glamour girl."

A dame in his car. A dame in his car.

Mary leaned forward.

"You'd need to watch him. My mother was telling me ..."

Mary Trimble's mother was a notorious gossip often seen standing in her street with a cluster of women around her. She always stood with her arms folded and her head bent to one side as she discussed the latest scandal of the town. Suddenly Mary looked like her mother. Her voice had taken on a low confidential note, Kate could see her fleshy mouth parting, her tongue poised to eject its venom. She couldn't bear to listen to it.

"Did you hear a noise outside?"

Anything to deflect the poison. Ciara sat up on the bed then she stood up slowly, stretched and walked languidly to the window.

"There's a car outside. Jesus, it's him, it's Steele."

At first Kate thought she was joking, Steele never came to visit at night. But soon they heard the rattle of the letterbox and her mother's answering step in the hall.

"The fags," gasped Ciara and she ran around the bottom of the bed, bumping into Mary, grabbing past her for the saucer full of ash. Martha grabbed Ciara's cigarette and tearing frantically at the layers of curtain, tried to throw it through the window.

"The curtains," Kate screamed, waving her arms wildly. "Mind the curtains."

Already she could imagine her mother's horrified face as she stared at the curtains on the Protestant window. Ciara had touched the lace with the glowing end of her cigarette as she tried to open the top of the window. In seconds the hot tip had burnt a hole in the centre of the white lace. As the three girls stared at the burnt curtain the bedroom door burst open and Steele threw himself into the room. The smile of greeting froze on his face as he took in the scene. His eyes travelled from the cigarette butts in the saucer to the swirling smoke around the naked electric light bulb.

"Out".

He held the door open and as the two girls slunk quickly past him, sniggering nervously, he grabbed Ciara's cigarette and ground it viciously into the saucer.

"Thanks for calling, come again," Kate called feebly after them and began to cough.

Steele slammed the door behind them and walked over to the bed. There was no sound but the clatter of shoes on the stairs, the raised tone of surprise in Harriet's voice, the hurried "goodbyes" and then the front door slamming. Through the open window came the sound of voices full of outrage as the girls moved away from the window.

In the gathering darkness the old church brooded over the silent street. Steele stood with his back to Kate - she couldn't see his face.

"Do you realise how much it costs to cure one person of tuberculosis? The cost of x-rays, radiologists, laboratory technicians to mention but a few items? How do you expect me to continue to take an interest in your health when I turn my back for a moment and you do a stupid thing like that?"

He turned around to her for a moment.

"What sort of an eejit are you?" he shouted into her face.

There was a silence. He turned his back to her again and stood outlined against the fading light from the Catholic window. As she watched him resentfully she saw him raise his hand to his forehead then rub his eyes tiredly. This small gesture, combined with his uncharacteristic attitude of dejection, melted her heart towards him. She knew he worked night and day, fighting a continual battle against the ignorance and superstition of his patients and the bureaucracy of the authorities. He had even butted horns with the Catholic clergy. Catholics were always on the alert for any real or fancied insult to their beliefs. A few years previously a rumour had flashed through the town that Steele had ordered a priest from the bedside of a dying patient. Kate had come home from school and rushed in to tell her mother about it.

"Well, I suppose there must be something behind it." Harriet had said. "But I know that Robert Steele doesn't know the meaning of religious bigotry. He must have had the welfare of his patient in mind."

Kate had mentioned it to him one day when they were driving along a country lane.

"So you heard that old story," he had said laughing. "About big bad Steele with the horns and the tail."

"I knew it wasn't true."

"Oh, it's true alright. I did it before and I'd do it again. When I'm called to a patient who has a cardiac arrest, as the Americans are now calling a heart attack, it is my job to keep them in this world, not to despatch them to the next. Every second is vital. I asked Fr McGlinchy to leave the patient and my request drew the wrath of the Catholic clergy on top of my head. I don't see that I had any choice in the matter."

She began to understand why he had dismissed her two friends.

"I'm sorry," she said to his back. "But cigarette smoking is harmless, nobody can say that it's not."

"As far back as nineteen hundred and twelve an epidermatologist called Richard Dall produced conclusive evidence that cigarette smoking is a cause of pulmonary disease. There's research going on all the time. In the next few years I think we'll discover a shocking connection between smoking and lung cancer. Anyway, we'll forget what happened, I can't stay angry with you for long."

He sat down on the bed facing her. His body exuded warmth, his breath alcohol. Kate sat up and looked at him in surprise. He began to laugh.

"So you smell the brandy. Don't forget I'm not working all the time. Actually I delivered a baby this afternoon to a woman in the country. When the baby was born it couldn't breathe, the respiratory passages were clogged with mucous. The White Baby Syndrome it's called and you can imagine yourself how potentially serious it could be. I asked the woman's husband for a sup of brandy, I drank it and breathed it into the infant's mouth. It's an old-fashioned remedy, you won't find it in the textbooks but it worked like a charm. The tiny respiratory passages dilated, he began to cough and expelled the mucous - he was breathing properly in no time."

He leaned towards her.

"I can see your eyes dilating now."

He stood up ready to leave.

"What did I come up here for?"

He scratched his head comically.

"Oh yes, you have an x-ray on Monday. I'll call for you at two in the afternoon and bring you to the Chest Hospital."

As he reached the door she shouted after him.

"I saw you down the town with a blonde today."

He stiffened with surprise, a flicker of annoyance crossed his face, then he pulled the door open and smiled over at her.

"Did you now ... that was my sister."

When he had gone she lay back on the pillow, crimson with embarrassment. What a thing to shout at him ... as if she owned him. Still it was nice to know that it was only his sister in the car.

It was a long time later and she was almost asleep when she remembered Steele telling her he was an only child.

* * *

She sat on a chair facing the radiologist who pointed to a chart on the wall. The shadows on the chart looked like a mountain range but they weren't. The chart was a photograph of her lungs.

"Now," he said to her, "You will notice that this area is different - the shadow is deeper."

She stared and couldn't see anything different about it but she smiled and nodded. As she looked closer she thought she saw a small round hole going right through the x-ray surrounded by a deep circular shadow. It was probably where the disease had attacked her lung and the area had calcified around it. She was going to ask him but she was afraid that he and his nurse might burst into peals of derisive laughter. He came over and sat at the desk opposite her.

"Would you like to be up and about again?"

"You mean all day, not just a few hours?"

He nodded and smiled, his lined face looked tired.

"It's nice to have good news occasionally, in your case it's very good news. We didn't expect such a complete recovery so soon."

"Soon! It's been two years."

"My dear girl, your blood sedimentation rate was sky high and we weren't able to bring it down. For no apparent reason it suddenly dropped to normal. I don't understand why."

Kate looked past him and through the window behind him where she could see Steele hunched over the wheel of his car waiting for her.

I understand why, she thought.

Nurse Patterson stood beside him unsmiling, watching her with shrewd brown eyes. She was an ugly woman, small and stocky with thick muscular legs. She was slightly younger than Kate's mother but had known her years ago when they attended the same Sunday School. When she came to King Street to check on Kate's progress she would sit downstairs with Harriet, drinking tea and talking guardedly to Harriet of people she once knew. Kate would kneel on the landing above and watch her mother as she sat, pale with emotion, grateful for crumbs of information about her former friends. The nurse would throw meagre scraps and with knowledge and mockery on her face watch Harriet beg for more.

"Imagine all Somerville's pigs dying," Harriet would say for days afterwards. Or again, "Betty Watson with only six months to live. They say she's as yellow as a duck's foot."

She would shake her head sadly, longing to be involved in the demise of Betty Watson. By running away with a Catholic, she had broken with her clan and was now like somebody locked outside her home having an occasional peep in through the window and seeing a one-dimensional, distorted image of the kaleidoscope of their lives.

Now, Dr Anderson fiddled with a pencil.

"Have you given any thought to your future? Decided what you want to work at?"

"I would like to be a nurse ... if I was strong enough."

"Of course you'd be strong enough. Will you go back to school first?"

"I don't have to, I passed my 'O' levels before I became ill."

"You'll go to the Royal?"

Nurse Patterson threw him a reproachful look. The Royal Victoria in Belfast was not known to favour Catholic girls as student nurses. In every Preliminary Training School there were only one or two token Catholics. There were no Catholic medical students. Dr Anderson remembered and turned a deep embarrassed red. He stood up and walked over to the window. Nurse Patterson turned her sallow face to Kate.

"There's always the Mater Hospital."

Keep to your own side of the road, she was saying.

Dr Anderson turned from the window.

"How will you get back home? Did you come out by taxi?"

"Dr Steele drove me out."

Why do you ask, she wondered, when you are looking straight at his car?

The doctor and nurse did not move from their positions, but Kate sensed a heightening of tension in the room. They seemed to be quiet, alert and waiting. She stood facing them, anxious to be dismissed.

Dr Anderson coughed.

"Well, goodbye for now. Tell Robert he'll have that report in the post. I'll have you back for x-ray in two months."

She climbed into the car smiling with delight. Steele looked at her and held his hand up.

"No, don't tell me now. Wait until we go somewhere nice and then tell me."

As they drove away a flash of white caught Kate's eye: looking up she saw a small squat figure watching them from the window of the clinic.

"Where are we going?"

"Today you decide ... we'll go anywhere you like."

"A few years ago a gang of us used to walk out to the country to an old mill. There was a mill pond, a river, and behind it a forest. I'd love to see it again."

He nodded and smiled.

"Crinnon's mill. I know it well, you have an eye for beauty."

* * *

They walked along the track towards the mill pond. At the edge they stopped. The pond was smooth and clear, it mirrored their faces as they peered in.

"It's very deep."

"It's bottomless," she said

"How could an intelligent girl like you say such a ridiculous thing? It's a mill pond for Christ's sake, probably man-made, you've been to school, you've studied physical geography. It's deep alright but ..."

"No, not this pond, it's really bottomless. It's the one pool we never tried to swim in...it goes on to infinity."

He squinted across at her.

"Nothing goes on to infinity. Everything that we see is in a state of change. Even the mountains and the sea are not static and everything has an end, a few years in medicine teaches you that."

"The loss of God goes on to infinity, that's what hell really is. Not the pain of fire but the loss of God."

"And heaven?"

"The love of God to infinity."

"And you believe that? Do you not think some busybody thought that up to frighten us into being good? Personally, I don't believe there is a hell."

They looked at each other, standing apart, shocked at each other's beliefs, the road of their different cultures an infinity between them. They left the pond and crossed the open field towards the river, stepping aside to avoid tufts of grass, they bumped into each other. Steele slid his arm around her waist.

"That's better, now put your arm around my waist."

They walked along the river bank, with arms entwined like lovers. Shyly she leaned her head towards his shoulder but suddenly he pulled away.

"What am I thinking about? I must be hankering after my lost youth."

They came to the edge of the pine trees. They stopped and stared into the woods where the trees were closely woven, dark and private. The forest floor was a carpet of pine needles. Shafts of sunlight beamed warm rays through chinks in the thick roof. The air was heavy with the scent of resin. Kate plunged into the forest, turned and held her hand out towards Steele.

"Come on."

But he stood at the edge of the trees and shook his head.

She walked towards him, took his hand and pulled him gently. He disengaged his hand. They stood close together and stared at each other. Kate began to tremble.

"Oh Kate."

His arms were around her waist and he drew her close to him. She could feel his heart thumping, felt the heat of his lips as they touched hers. She put her arms around his neck and strained towards him. Suddenly he drew back and pushed her violently away from him. He cut straight across the field towards his car. Kate stood at the edge of the forest, her head bent forward, hands covering her face. Gradually she regained control and stopped trembling. She began to walk slowly back to the car. When she came to the mill pond she stopped and once again stared into its glassy depths.

"It is bottomless," she said.

She passed around its edge and trailed her feet slowly towards the car. Steele was huddled in the driver's seat with his head bent forward. She opened the door and sat in beside him. He ignored her. He had opened a tin of fishing flies and was sorting through them. He held a large fly up to the light and the sun shimmered an iridescent blue and green on its fragile feathers. With a gasp of delight she reached her hand to touch it.

"Leave it alone."

His voice was harsh as he replaced the fly in the box and snapped the lid shut.

"On the back of each of these flies there's a vicious hook, it would cut right through your hand."

"I see."

They sat in silence for a while.

"Did your mother never teach you the facts of life?"

She looked at him in surprise.

"You did."

"I taught you the biological facts but there are more subtle things. Things that a young girl should know by instinct. For instance, you shouldn't make a habit of dragging men into the woods."

She sat silent, embarrassed.

"I'm only human and a weak man at that - I think you're far too innocent and trusting."

He turned around and stroked her hair gently then tucked it behind her ears.

"Don't you realise, pet, that as soon as I saw those woods all I wanted was to bring you into them and make love to you? And that's a job for some other lucky man - not for me."

* * *

She tossed and turned in her bed at night terrified of her thoughts. Innocent and trusting. The words beat into her brain. She knew he was the one too innocent and naive to see into the depths of her black heart. She knew he was married and wished his wife no harm but he had placed himself as a crutch she could lean on to escape from the grave, now she was totally dependent on the crutch - she didn't know how to take the next step to achieve personal independence. Soon she would be well enough to make her own way through life. The thought terrified her. At night she lay awake thinking of ways she could stay in his life forever. Most of her solutions necessitated the absence of his wife. In the moments before sleep, when imagination ran riot, uncontrolled by reason, Mrs Steele died a thousand times. She was run over by innumerable buses, killed in plane crashes, became victim of rare and fatal diseases.

When Kate saw her in the flesh, radiant and healthy, her evil thoughts never troubled her, she did not willingly think these things, they rose up from the dark recesses of her mind where noxious thoughts bubbled and fermented.

As the time of her confinement drew near Pamela Steele came down to the garden almost every day. Steele fussed over her, setting up her deckchair, bringing her magazines, fetching the old straw hat to shield her eyes from the sun. She always greeted Kate with the same vague smile, calling her by the wrong name, obviously well used to and tolerant of the friends of her eccentric husband. When she came down to spend afternoons in the garden, Steele would talk to her all the time, calling her constantly to look at what he had been doing in the garden, explaining his plans to her. On these days Kate was left alone wandering around the flowerbeds, bored and forgotten, trapped in a limbo between childhood and womanhood. One day early in Autumn he planted some shrubs and stood back to rub the clay from his hands and admire his handiwork. He was laughing and joking across to his wife who sat facing him. In a fit of pique and jealousy Kate stamped down from the edge of a flowerbed passing him needlessly and too close on the narrow path. She pretended to stumble and caught him around the waist to steady herself.

"Sorry," she mumbled.

Steele stopped talking in the middle of a sentence. From behind, Kate could see the deep flush spread across the back of his neck. His wife said nothing, but stared across at Kate, her eyebrows raised in surprise.

From behind Steele's shoulder Kate stared back at her and saw the other woman's face register puzzlement, then a gradual dawning of realisation. Kate saw her face pale to a sickly grey and they continued to stare at each other, their eyes locked in mutual antagonism.

Kate dropped her eyes first.

"I'll go on home now, it's getting late."

Chapter Six

As she walked home from the garden she knew she would have to change her life in some way so that she wouldn't meet Steele again. But how to accomplish this she did not know. There was nobody she could turn to. The groundwork for intimacy had never been laid between Kate and Harriet, their relationship as mother and daughter was barren. Kate knew that her only feeble effort at taking her mother into her confidence had failed, and that any other attempt would create embarrassment for both of them.

She would go to Confession and tell the priest. If God spoke through him as she had been taught, she would find out what she should do.

Kate knelt in the narrow plywood confession box. Panic made her throat dry and her head throb. Just as she was about to stand up and bolt through the door the grille that divided her from the priest opened abruptly.

"Bless me Father ..."

"Number of weeks since your last confession?"

She could see Fr McGlinchey's crewcut bent towards the door of the confession box. Light filtered through the cut-out design on the outside of the box and was beamed onto the wall behind him. He never glanced towards the wire mesh grille behind which she knelt. One hand strayed impatiently from his knee and quivered almost in the act of absolution. The other hand held the door of the grille ready to slide it shut as soon as she drew breath. Machine-gun McGlinchey they called him. He rattled off the absolution and spat out the penance without showing any interest in the sin. Everyone crowded to him for Confession and the row of penitents outside his box undulated along the seat in constant movement. She had picked him with care. She would fit her mortal sin in among the venial sins and he would never notice. She drew a quick shaking breath.

"It's a year since my last Confession."

In a society where people were encouraged to be shriven at least once a month this was remarkable. She sensed that the soutane-covered figure stiffened in the gloom but he resolutely kept his head down.

"I told lies to my mother. I was lazy and deceitful - on three occasions."

The head nodded approvingly, the hand moved into the air. She drew a deep breath.

"I've fallen in love with a married man."

There was a gasp and his head rose and peered through the grille at her. A shamrock of light appeared on his forehead. Her mother had always said that he was very handsome and looked like Alan Ladd. Now she saw that his skin was damp and sweaty with coarse open pores and that his eyes were small and suspicious.

As he began to question her, he strained towards her, sought her out and identified her in the gloom.

"This married man, has he children? ... Well?" he said impatiently when she did not answer.

"His wife is expecting a baby."

There was a silence and she felt that the priest was having difficulty in controlling his feelings of outrage.

"How often do you see him?"

"Almost every day."

"Does he know of your feelings?"

"Yes."

She was squirming now, lathered with sweat.

"He kisses you, of course?"

There was a silence. This was the Confessional and she had to tell the truth. Her voice was hoarse as she replied.

"Yes."

"How old are you?"

"Almost eighteen."

"And he is?"

"Thirty eight."

"Oh God."

The priest leaned forward and covered his face with his hands. His whole body seemed to slump into an appearance of dejection and despair.

What have I done to him, Kate thought in the continuing silence. She rubbed her hands together and waited. At last he straightened up.

"Have you told me everything? Did you have intercourse with this man?"

"No."

She could feel herself go weak all over. She felt degraded, glancing quickly towards him she saw a flash of contempt before it was quickly hidden. His face came close to hers and peered gimlet-eyed through the grille.

"Are you sure you're telling me the truth?"

"Yes,"

"Now listen to me carefully. You are in grave moral danger, a young girl at the mercy of an unscrupulous man. Now you must sever all connection with him immediately."

"I will have to see him sometimes."

There was a silence.

"Well, in that case I must refuse to grant you absolution."

Kate could feel her knees tremble. To be refused absolution meant that she was a sinner whose heinous act was so grave that even God could not forgive. She cowered in the corner of the box. She was in a court-room, she had been tried and convicted of a gross offence. Fr McGlinchey, the judge, was summing up and passing sentence.

"The sixth commandment condemning adultery encompasses more than the act itself. There are occasions of sin, giving in to evil thoughts, wilfully indulging in the company of someone who is committed to another. Things like this lead to temptation to commit grievous sin. You must avoid these things as you would avoid sin itself."

She sensed that he was talking about something

different to her gentle relationship with Steele. But she was too frightened to speak, to explain to him that she had come to see him for help and advice. At last she whispered,

"The only way I could promise not to see this man again is to go away."

There was a silence then.

"Well, if that is what you must do."

"I will never see him again."

"Do you promise God?"

"I promise."

At last he raised his hand and gave her absolution and told her to say the Rosary as a penance. As she rose stiffly to go, he said.

"Just a moment before you go."

She knelt down again.

"I am very concerned about your welfare. You have told me these things in the secrecy of the Confessional and I must respect the confidentiality of what you have divulged. I can only advise you, outside of here I cannot help you. Could you tell any of this to your mother?"

She shook her head.

"Your teachers?"

She thought of the remote figures with their pale ascetic faces. They were an enclosed order of nuns, some of her teachers had not been through the gates of the Convent for over thirty years.

"No."

"I can only advise you to go and see your doctor. This whole thing is obviously causing you great distress. He will respect the confidential nature of what you tell him and he may be able to get a counsellor for you. God bless you my child."

He slid the door over and she was alone. Even as she stood up to leave the Confessional she could hear a door slide open and the low voice of a penitent on the other side. She stumbled out of the box feeling strained and light-headed. A hundred bent heads were raised to stare at her. She was obviously a sinner worthy of notice. Fr McGlinchey kept nobody long without good reason. She knelt at the back of the church to say her penance.

"Oh, my God I am heartily sorry ..."

She stopped. She was not sorry, she thought. Steele had pulled her from an abyss of despair. He had taught her how to appreciate the beauty of the world around her and by his concern had taught her how to value herself as a human being. They had often talked about sorrow for sin in her doctrine class.

"What if you committed a sin and it was the nicest thing that ever happened to you?" Ciara asked Mother Laverty one day. "What would you do about sorrow then?"

"You would excite yourself to contrition."

So Kate began to think of all the hours she had spent with Steele when he should have been at home with his wife and she should have been sitting at the fire with her mother. She thought of the days when he had brought her fishing with him, the day in the country when he had climbed a tree to get her a piece of wild cherry blossom. Now she was walking with him through the heather, following closely behind him as he beat a path through the whins so that they wouldn't cut her legs, again he held her hand while she stepped carefully over flat stones that spanned a river. But there was no sense of contrition, only an almost unbearable sense of loneliness and loss. There

was also a feeling of guilt, a sense that she had done
Steele a terrible injustice by saying anything to Fr
McGlinchey about him. She finished her penance
quickly and left the church. As she left by the main
door she bumped into Martha Grey coming from the
side door. She looked at Kate with interest.

"You must have some powerful big sins. I thought
you'd never come out of that box."

"I have a secret lover, a married man."

She looked at Kate shrewdly.

"You don't even know any married men, except Dr
Steele of course." Then she looked at Kate doubtfully.
"What's lover-boy's name?"

"Lean closer and I'll tell you."

Martha leaned close to Kate, her mouth hanging
open. Close to her Kate could hear her excited
breathing.

"Skiboo."

She laughed good-humoredly and walked beside
Kate linking her arm through hers.

"There's a hop in the town hall tonight, would you
like to come? It's only half a crown to get in."

"I wouldn't be allowed."

"Tell your mother that you're staying with me.
Make up some yarn. She'll never know you were at a
dance."

When Kate asked, Harriet fidgeted with indecision.

"Whose house?"

"Martha Grey's. Her mother asked me if I would
stay and keep her company. She has to stay in her
Grandmother's tonight. She's very ill."

"Old Mrs McLarnan's been dead these years."

"The father's mother." How quickly, how expertly
she lied, she knew that not a muscle in her face

changed.

"Oh, I don't know her."

She looked at her daughter doubtfully, feeling she should object but not knowing why. Kate stared back at her wide-eyed and innocent.

"Well, just this once and only because Mrs Grey asked you. And mind, don't ever ask me again."

Kate felt a stab of guilt. Already new sins were beginning to stain her soul which she felt must be like a shining white bone somewhere inside her. When the time came to leave the house she didn't dare to change her clothes but collected a cardigan from upstairs and furtively put a comb in one pocket and a lipstick in the other.

"What about your pyjamas?"

"Martha said she'd lend me a pair."

Martha opened the front door and looked her up and down.

"What did you bring to wear?"

She saw Kate's face redden.

"Your blouse is lovely and so is your dirndl skirt but you need to look a bit more glamorous for the hop. C'mon, our Eileen has some nice clothes."

She brought Kate straight upstairs to the bedroom and began to rummage through the wardrobe.

"There."

She threw a black satin blouse onto the bed.

"And there."

It was followed by a long black straight skirt with a slit in the back. Martha crawled around under the bed and threw a pair of black strapped sandals towards her one by one.

"Now get into that, and hurry. We'll have to be out of here before she comes home and catches us wearing them."

Kate removed her plain shirt-waister blouse and slipped into the black creation. Her senses were assailed with a pleasant smell of perfume and then the fainter more intimate smell of another woman's body. With a feeling of revulsion she began to unbutton the blouse. Martha came up behind her.

"What are you doing? Keep it on, it looks nearly as nice on you as it does on our Eileen and she's always rushed off her feet at the dances. Look at me, I'm wearing her good red dress."

She spun around, her hair, newly washed and shining, floating behind her.

"When we start to work we'll be able to afford clothes like these."

"I'll have my wardrobe full and I'll burn everything that I own now," Kate said, thinking of the grey flannel skirt and the flat laced shoes. They left the house and passed through the town barely moving in their long tight skirts. They came to the group of men who forever stood four deep at the corner below the dancehall who parted ranks reluctantly to let them walk through They picked their way with exaggerated care through the blobs of spit and cigarette butts. The men kept their heads modestly lowered towards their shuffling feet, but their eyes were slyly raised towards the girls and when they had passed by they began to whistle and shout.

"Hey, darling , this fella wants a word with you."

"Oh, Mammy buy me the doll with the black hair."

Martha and Kate had walked along this footpath for as long as they could remember, coming to and from school and going on endless messages for their mothers, but until they wore their borrowed plumes nobody had ever whistled after them.

"Corner boys," said Martha looking at Kate, her eyes shining with delight. "As if we'd stoop so low to lift so little."

Kate tiptoed daintily beside her friend cocooned in the web of her confidence, until they came to the door of the dancehall and she baulked with fear.

"I can't go in there," she said. She had begun to sweat and could feel a rushing sound in her ears.

Martha pushed her forward.

"Don't be silly. You can't back out now."

They paid for their tickets at the door and, caught in a babel of voices, were drawn up the carpeted stairs to the music above. As Kate reached the top of the stairs and faced the shadowy dancehall, she could see entwined figures locked in the pulsating throb of the music. The beat of the music beckoned her. She could feel herself shiver with excitement as half-forgotten memories of the weekend dances in King Street flooded through her. At last she was part of it all, no longer outside looking in. She almost ran to the dancehall. Martha caught her by the arm.

"We can't go in yet. We have to go to the cloakroom first."

"What for?"

Martha rolled her eyes.

"To get ready, what do you think?"

Kate wondered what they had been doing before they left, prinking in front of the mirror, tweezing stray hairs from their eyebrows, combing their hair in every imaginable style. But there seemed to be a ritual about dancing and tonight she was being initiated. She followed Martha obediently into the cloakroom. Anxious faces peered above and below

them as they tried to hold their places in front of the
glass. Eyebrows were plucked, faces rouged and a
few daring girls were spiking their eyelashes with
thick black mascara. Kate put more lipstick on,
combed her hair and stood back to wait for Martha.
At first glance the room seemed to be full of friendly
chatting girls but soon she saw that this was an
illusion. The Protestant girls had collected at one side
of the mirror, the Catholics at the other. There was no
hostility, no poaching on each other's territory. But
the invisible glass was there and nobody seemed to
be able to communicate with the people on the other
side. Even as she stood watching she saw a Catholic
girl walk down to the centre of the mirror and call to
her friend.

"Come on down here, there's nobody here,"
ignoring the dozens of girls crammed like sardines on
the other side of her. She was not joking, for her the
people on the other side of her did not exist. They
moved into the dancehall.

"Did I tell you I'm meeting Louis Murphy here?"

"Who is Louis Murphy?"

"He's a new teacher in the Tech. He's twenty-five,"
Martha added proudly. "Look, there he is, I'd better
go over to him, he's watching out for me."

She turned to walk away but Kate pulled her back.

"Why didn't you tell me you had to meet someone
here, what am I supposed to do if you go off with
him?"

Martha gave her a mock admiring glance.

"Sure, you'll have the feet danced off you and don't
worry, we'll come back now and again to see that
you're alright. I'll not leave the hall without you," she
added virtuously.

"I can't dance."

Martha sighed.

"What a wet blanket, can't you shuffle around, who'll know the difference? Oh, by the way, don't get up with any British soldiers."

"Why not?"

Martha shrugged.

"Nobody dances with them, well, none of our kind. Not that they'll bother you. They usually dance with the girls who live near the army barracks, they know them, they're all prods."

"What do I say if they ask me to dance?"

"Just say that you've promised the dance to someone else - they'll take the hint."

She was trying to escape now but Kate hung grimly to the belt of her red dress.

"How will I know them?"

"Oh for God's sake, you'll know them. They look ... English. They have an army look about them, clean and scrubbed."

"And now we will have a slow waltz." The band struck up and above their heads a silver globe began to twirl, slowly throwing patterns of light and colour over the dim hall. Kate stood near a cluster of girls pretending she was in their company. As the men crossed the room towards them, they began to chatter frantically, trying to show a complete lack of concern.

"May I have this dance?"

"Would you like to dance?"

The chosen girls moved off smirking with pleasure, the crowd along the walls thinned. Soon she stood by herself at the side of the dance floor, a beacon of loneliness in her black shiny blouse. She stared in front of her, longing to be invisible. Martha passed by

her dancing with a small bowlegged man whose
black wiry hair sprung from his head in a comical
parody of surprise. Surely she couldn't like him, that
ugly little man, Kate thought. But what would
Martha think of her feelings for Steele, a middle-aged
man with thinning hair? From the dance floor she
waved towards Kate and continued her conversation.
Kate slunk back and thankfully sat down on one of
the plush seats which lined the walls. The dance
finished and everybody returned to their places, Kate
sat and craned her head for Martha but there was no
sign of her. Another dance was announced, this time
a quickstep. The floor filled up, she watched the
dancers with interest. To her surprise, she was
beginning to recognise some faces. Miss Henry, the
maths teacher, looking naked without her cap and
gown, passed by in the clutches of a bald middle-
aged man. Her gaunt yellow face was incongruously
painted with twin spots of rouge. Kate watched in
fascination as her long thin feet moved in geometric
designs across the floor. Maureen O'Toole from the
fish shop wheezed past staring at her partner with
her protuberant eyes, and sweeping along behind her
came Jerry Kennedy, the council workman who
pushed his brush through the oil-filled puddles of
King Street every Monday morning. She noticed that
Petie Nixon and his girlfriend kept to the outside of
the throng and at each corner they executed a few
intricate steps. Petie wore a yellow silk cravat, his tan
sports-jacket had two slits in the back and bounced
rhythmically every time he whirled around.

"May I have this dance?"

He had spoken twice and the girl beside her
nudged her before she realised that he was

addressing her. She looked up into a face with clear hazel eyes, peaches and cream skin and a blond crewcut. Everything about him, from his black shiny shoes to his fair cropped hair spoke of an army man. Alarm bells began to ring in her head. Was she supposed to say that she had promised the dance to somebody? It was obvious that she was not in any great demand as the dance was almost over and she was still sitting with the wallflowers.

"I can't dance," she blurted out.

"I'm not very good either. Maybe we can learn together."

His eyes had a pleading look. Don't let me down they were saying. She stood up and moved with him out onto the dance floor, where she discovered that he was an excellent dancer. She fumbled along behind him trying to concentrate on the steps.

"I've never been to a dance before."

"That doesn't surprise me," he said. "How old are you? Sixteen?"

"Almost eighteen."

"Relax," he whispered into her ear as the floor filled up and they were jostled closer. "Just listen to the music, try to get the rhythm of it and forget about your feet. No, don't dance on your toes, and let me lead. Let yourself go and follow me around the floor."

Under her partner's expert tuition she was able to follow his steps, soon her feet were treading happily around the dance floor and she realised that she was beginning to enjoy herself. She had time to take stock of her partner. He was taller than Steele, her hands had to reach higher to touch his shoulders. His skin was much fairer, he was younger. Steele is my yardstick now, she thought, I don't see men as tall but taller, not young but younger. She smiled grimly to herself, she had a long way to go before she forgot him.

"A penny for them."

She pulled herself together with an effort.

"I'm sorry, I was daydreaming. You see, I'm going to work in England soon. I heard your accent and I was wondering what part you come from. It's not London, it's the North of England but not Liverpool.."

"Manchester," he said.

"You miss it, I suppose?"

"Can't wait to get back, I've been here for nearly two years, doing my national service ..."

The music rose on a crescendo and the dance finished. As she went to move away she felt a tight grip on her arm.

"May I have the next dance?"

And when she agreed he said, "Well stay here and talk to me, then I won't have to go looking for you."

He offered her a cigarette.

Keith was his name and he told her he was a draughtsman.

"Will it be difficult to get a job when you go back?"

He shook his head.

"My old firm will be taking me back."

As the next dance was called out and he led her onto the floor, he said, "Have you any particular reason for going to London? It can be a very lonely place. You should consider going to a hospital in the North of England. There are some good hospitals around Manchester. My sister's in the Royal Infirmary. I'll give you the address, it's quite near my home."

The Royal Infirmary, she thought. I'll write there.

When the dance was nearly over he said to her.

"Why don't we stay together for the rest of the evening? We both seem to be on our own."

"If you don't mind having your feet trodden all over."

"It would be a pleasure to show you a few more steps, you're a very apt pupil."

The next dance was a tango and she backed away.

"That's a very complicated dance. I wouldn't be able to do it."

"You never know what you can do until you try."

The passionate music of *Jealousy* throbbed through the hall. Keith held her firmly and very close. She forgot about Martha, and the local townspeople dancing around her. She was keeping perfect time to the music, lost in the rhythm of the dance.

She felt a tap on her shoulder.

She turned around and looked into Martha's face.

"Come over here."

Keith guided her through the crowd and over to the side of the hall. Martha pulled her away, out of earshot.

"He's a British soldier."

"It wouldn't be too hard to guess that," Kate giggled. "The hair."

Martha was not amused.

"I asked you not to get up with any of them. The hall's full of them tonight. There is a lot of resentment about so many of them being here - one or two of them we could take. I told you that our sort don't dance with them - well, not the ones with any pride in them."

"Yes, well I'm different. I see no harm in it."

Martha shrugged.

"You have to do what everyone else does or take the consequences."

"I couldn't refuse to dance with him."

"Why not? Everyone else did. We were watching him, he went right down that row of girls and everyone refused to get up with him until he came to you, ye big eejit. Now I've been told to warn you to get rid of him - immediately."

"And if I don't?"

"Do you want to be beaten up on your way home, or him to be beaten up?"

"Nobody would do that."

But her heart had given a lurch of fright.

"Wouldn't they? If this was Belfast you'd have your head shaved. Or you might be tarred and feathered."

"I don't believe you."

They stood glaring at each other.

"C'mon, get your coat, we're going home."

"I'll have to tell him."

"Tell him nothing, just walk past him, cut him dead."

"But he's been very nice."

"He's a Brit, for God's sake, what does he expect? You'll be doing him a favour as well as yourself if you just bale out without looking at him."

Kate looked at Martha doubtfully and saw that she was nervous and agitated, anxious to leave the dancehall as quickly as possible.

"Louis will run us home in his car, we'll leave quietly before the crowd comes out, it'll be safer."

Who had told Martha?

She looked around. The tango had finished and people were standing around in laughing, chatting groups. At the door leading to the back stairs minerals were being served and a few couples had gathered around the makeshift counter. The men were jostling each other playfully, the girls were in a giggling group. Nobody was taking any notice of Kate, most of the people here barely knew her name. But with a shiver she realised that her feeling of anonymity was an illusion. Here as in King Street people watched.

She thought of her mother protecting herself from prying eyes behind layers of curtains.

Is this what would happen to her?

No. Soon she would go away and leave it all behind. She would make a fresh start.

"All right, I'll come."

Keith had stood politely by as Kate and Martha had argued under their breaths. Now she glanced over at him. He was standing very erect, a soldier on parade, but she could see that his face was crimson with embarrassment. From nowhere a group of British soldiers had appeared to watch and protect. Behind Martha Louis stood looking over at Kate, his schoolmaster's mouth pursed with disapproval. In the breeze from the fan above, his hair waved like antennae towards the British soldiers. She lowered her head with shame and passed Keith without a glance.

* * *

Once she had thought of her bedroom as a prison cell. Now that she was free to go where she liked she seldom left it. In here among the familiar belongings she was safe, away from the complications of taking up the thread of life outside.

The day was endlessly long.

Every morning her mother wakened her with her breakfast, as she had done when she was sick. She went to the windows, raised the blinds, drew the curtains back and re-pleated them while Kate sipped her tea. When she had gone Kate would lie and listen to the morning sounds in the street below. Petie's arrival at the shop with fresh bread set the whole street into motion. Kate would creep down to the bottom of the bed and watch from her window as doors opened cautiously and old faces peered out. The stone steps of the houses were carefully negotiated, walking sticks tapped their slow way along as crooked feet walked the crooked pavement to the shop. They gathered around Petie, attracted like old tattered moths to his light-hearted personality. He chatted and joked with them, singling them out by name. When her mother crossed over to the shop, they fell silent, she was the only woman who didn't wear an apron. They greeted her with reserve and stepped aside to make way for her at the counter. There was an uneasy silence until she left.

Kate would hear the tea being made and then she would listen to her mother singing as she worked around the kitchen. From her bed she would watch the crows wheeling around the turret of the old Cathedral.

"Soon I'll be gone to England and all this will be just a memory."

She had seen advertisements in the *Irish News* looking for young Irish girls to train as nurses. By a coincidence one of them was the Royal Infirmary. She went out to see Dr Anderson in the Chest Hospital and asked him if he thought that she would be fit for nursing.

"Well let's face it," he said laughing. "You should have a damned good immunity to any tubercular infection. I will put a covering note on your application explaining what you had. I don't think that it will go against you."

In the meantime she lay upstairs on her bed and stared at the ceiling. When she heard a car she would crawl down the bed to the window. In a street where so many people were old and sick the doctors visited regularly. Twice she saw Steele coming from old Mrs Teevan's house across the road. Each time he stood at the edge of the pavement and looked over at their front door, hesitated, then climbed into his car and drove off and each time Kate watched with a sickening feeling of disappointment as the retreating tail-lights of his car winked back at her. She would come down for her dinner and sit at the fire reading, while her mother cleared up and washed the dishes. The fire was always too hot, it sapped her will and her energy. She lay in the leather chair feeling bloated and lethargic.

Sometimes she would force herself to her feet, get her bicycle from the shed in the back yard and go out for a spin. She cycled around the country roads where she had been with Steele. She went back out to the old mill pond and stared into its glossy depths.

Oh what doth ail thee Knight at arms, alone and
palely loitering.
The sedge has withered from the lake and no birds sing.

Was it such a short time since she had learned that, rhymed it off and recited it with the class in a meaningless singsong voice?

One late afternoon after she had hung around the

house all day she walked out to her mother in the kitchen.

"I'm going out for a wee while."

"Aye alright," Harriet said. "A wee breath of fresh air will do you good."

Harriet knew that she had nowhere to go and Kate lowered her gaze from the pity she could see in her mother's eyes. She knew she was concerned about her, worried about her future. But Kate still found it impossible to confide in her, to penetrate the immense barrier of reserve that she had built around herself. Once or twice she had made an effort to reach her but the glass was there and she felt like some witless idiotic creature who mouthed at her in some unintelligible language from a distant planet. Now she went out and pulled the string in the letter box to close the front door carefully behind her. Harriet didn't like her to slam it. She said it shook the whole house and left her trembling to the core for the rest of the day.

When she turned around to walk up the street she saw Steele's car parked on the road above the house. The old trembling turned her legs to jelly as she walked towards it. He opened the door as she came along and she climbed in. They drove off without speaking - she sat silently beside him and breathed in the familiar medical smell that always seemed to cling to him. She stole a look towards him. They were driving towards the setting sun and the reflected radiance was on his face. Her heart raced almost out of control as she saw the dark skin, the upward curl of his long eyelashes. He turned and looked towards her but he did not return her tremulous smile.

"You didn't come down for the results of your last x-ray."

"I know that, but I'm alright. I feel fine."

She saw a twitch of annoyance on his face

"You always check back - right?"

"Was there something wrong with the x-ray?"

"It was alright as it happened, but you seem to have a cavalier attitude to the people who helped you to get well. Without a word of explanation you stopped coming to the garden."

They were out in the country now. He had slowed the car almost to a crawl and he pulled over onto the side of the road and parked on the grass verge under some trees.

"I seem to have a lot to do these days."

He sat back and closed his eyes. Close to him she saw that he looked deathly tired. It would be so easy to reach over put her arms around him..

"You lie too glibly it demeans you, insults our friendship. There are very few things worth lying over."

He opened his eyes and looked straight at her.

"Would it be such an awful thing to tell me the truth?"

She could feel her hands shaking. She slid them behind her on the seat and stared through the windscreen.

"I think you know what the reason is."

"Maybe I do," he said more gently.

They had parked on a hill. Below them, the river lay still, a reflection of the rosy sky was streaked across its glassy face. They sat without speaking and watched the changing colours of the sky, the unbelievable shades of violet, orange and red.

Turner didn't exaggerate, she wanted to say.

But trying to impress him didn't seem to matter any more. In the massive silence of the evening they were both infinitely small and unimportant, two specks of matter thrown together for a time and already feeling the might that would tear them apart. She turned towards him and he was looking at her. He leaned forward and lifted her hand gently. She felt the heat of his breath on her palm and thought that he was going to kiss it. She closed her eyes. But instead he said,

"You would need to take better care of your hands, keep your nails shorter - it's more hygienic."

He still seemed to hover somewhere between father and lover.

She wanted to say that her mother had made her black-lead the stove that morning, that the dirt had got under her finger nails and that she couldn't remove it.

But he knew when she was lying. She pulled her hand away and opened her eyes. He was leaning forward, his face close to hers. She pulled back from him and said quickly.

"Did I tell you that I'm going away to live in England soon?"

He sat back on his seat and looked at her, stunned.

"I'm going to train for nursing."

He began to laugh.

"You're not suited to nursing, you're far too sensitive. And you've been very ill. No, we'll think of a more suitable occupation ..."

"Dr Anderson says I would be well enough."

"You're saying that you've applied for the job

without even discussing it with me and that you told him - a man you barely know?"

She flinched from the hurt look in his eyes.

She tried to explain.

"I needed a covering letter from him, when I sent the application away. Now they want something from you. They'll be writing to you."

"And if you don't get the job?"

She shrugged.

"I'll get another. What does it matter?"

He sat with his head bent forward, a brooding expression on his face.

"Christ, Kate, what's bringing you to England? You'll die with loneliness." He tapped the steering wheel as he always did when he was thinking. Then he turned around.

"Don't go, not to England. Look, I've been thinking. What if I try to get you into the Royal in Belfast? It's near home. It's not too late to change your mind."

Temptation tried her. How she would love to work in the Royal, she would only be twenty miles away, she would be able to see him ... then Fr McGlinchey's face loomed before her.

You must never see this man again.

So she thought of all the Catholic girls she knew who were longing to get into the Royal Victoria to train for nursing but they never had a chance. She thought of all the letters of application painstakingly written, laying out precious achievements only to receive the time-worn reply: "No vacancies at present."

And Steele could walk roughshod over all the hopes and prayers and get her in to train because he was an influential Protestant.

"No, I want to get away from this country."

And now she knew that she meant it.

There was silence. He turned around, took her face in his hands, kissed her gently.

"I love your company," he whispered. "I love being with you."

With a sigh she laid her head on his shoulder. He stroked her hair gently.

"We'll probably never be alone together again."

In his voice there was a little sadness, a tinge of regret, not the ocean of loneliness that was engulfing her.

And even in his statement was the acknowledgment that their relationship would soon be a thing of the past. He drew her close to him, kissed her trembling lips, and she knew that neither of them could ever fool themselves again that their relationship was one of friendship.

Just as she knew that she was right to go away.

But it was hard to leave. They sat still, caught in a web of unreality, watching the sun set clouds on fire before it was remorselessly pulled below the rim of the horizon. Then as the moon rose to light the darkening sky, Steele switched the engine on and they drove home in silence along deserted roads.

Kate pulled the string in the front door and passed her mother in a trance. From a great distance, she could see Harriet standing at her chair watching her as she shook her head at the offer of supper. She undressed slowly, stiffly and climbed into the cold clean bed.

Almost immediately she fell into a dreamless sleep.

* * *

As soon as she wakened she knew that the rhythm of the day was different.

She listened.

She could always guess the time of the day by the sounds in the street below. Today there was no noise at all. A strange silence hung over the street. She could hear a low murmur of voices but they came from downstairs. Harriet had a visitor. She crawled down the bed to the window and saw that the wee shop across was closed, the windows shuttered. She felt a shock of surprise and then realised that she had slept right through the morning and that today was Wednesday, and halfday closing for all the shops in the town.

She padded out to the landing and knelt down to peep through the rails to see who her mother's visitor was. Harriet was sitting at the round table talking to Nurse Patterson. They were deeply engrossed in their conversation and didn't notice Kate kneeling above them.

"Why did she wait until she was forty to have her first baby?" her mother was saying. "I mean with him a doctor, they knew the risks."

"These people are too fond of a good time," the nurse was prim-mouthed and disapproving. "Having a family is the last thing that they think about."

What had happened when she was asleep?

She crept back to her room and climbed into the still-warm bed. She pulled the bedclothes over her head, shutting out the light, and curled herself into a ball. Here she was safe from everything but thoughts and they were enough to drive her mad as they churned around inside her head.

Mrs Steele was dead.

Kate had willed her dead and while she was asleep her vile wish had come true, she was as guilty of her death as if she had killed her with her own hands. She lay there wallowing in misery. No, that was not true. That was a pagan belief and had no part in her Christian faith. But she had disobeyed the instructions of a priest in Confession, and an evil thing had happened. Her head began to spin. A pinpoint of light appeared at the end of a dark tunnel. It moved slowly towards her until it loomed in front of her forming now into a pair of lips. The mouth full and purple opened and spoke.

"You have broken the ninth commandment," said Fr McGlinchey.

She sat bolt upright in the bed and threw the clothes back. She couldn't bear to stay here any longer, she would have to go down and face the music. From the landing above she could see the women downstairs whispering as she tiptoed to and from the bathroom. Slowly she washed and dressed, then carefully came down the stairs. The two women looked up towards her. Her mother smiled.

"If you get a cup there's a wee drop of tea in the pot. It should still be warm. I didn't like to disturb you, you were out for the count."

She lifted the tea-cosy and felt the pot with the palm of her hand. Nurse Patterson stared at her with cold Calvinistic eyes. Kate went over to the mirror which hung on the wall beside the window and began to comb her hair. The mirror was old and some of the silver was missing from the back. It gave her face a blotched appearance.

"Is Mrs Steele dead?"

She was surprised when the face in the mirror spoke. The three women stared at the mirror in shocked silence. The face looking back from the glass twisted its mouth comically, snickered and giggled.

"Indeed she's not dead," said Harriet.

"She's as fit as a fiddle," said the Nurse. "It was the baby who died."

Her hair was growing quickly. The curl at the back of her neck was too long. She fixed it carefully into place. The face that looked at her from the mirror had changed and was now sweet and smooth, unlined and unformed, too young to show the turmoil raging within. Behind her spotted reflection she could see the nurse watch her, a swift appraising woman's look shrewdly assessing the points of another. The expression on her face was cold and hostile. Kate stepped back from the mirror and moved slowly to the door.

"Are you not having a bite to eat? You can't run out now, nurse came up to have a word with you."

But already Kate was nodding and bowing, sliding across the room, her hand reaching for the brass door-knob.

"It's alright dear." said the nurse with a false smile. "Your mother says you're keeping well."

She nodded, trying to grip the handle of the door, turning it with slow fumbling movements.

"We'll have you out for x-ray in a few weeks but we'll notify you. You're very pale, I notice."

"Surely you're not going out like that?" Harriet's voice was shrill with annoyance. "Bare legs and sandals? In October?"

But Kate continued to grin idiotically at them until she was through the door and had closed it, blotting them out. She walked quickly through the town. She hated to see it like this with bare streets and shuttered shops. She always felt that everyone in the town was away somewhere doing exciting things while she was left wandering around with nowhere to go.

She loved the old town on fair day when the streets were full of bustle, and the traders set up their stalls in the market area, selling flowers, piglets and day-old chicks. She was happy walking through crowds of country people watching cattle skidding through the streets, carts spilling hay. When she was young and Harriet sent her for messages, she used to stand for hours leaning with her back to the wall of a pub in the Market Square listening to the voice of the old City, the honking of cars, the lowing of cattle and the nasal whine of the old tinker who made her way, hand-outstretched, through the ruddyfaced cattle dealers.

She turned down the street where Steele lived, the house stood in shadow - old and barren. A Protestant Georgian house, in a Protestant street. The front door was shut, the tall narrow windows were lashed with curtains, lidded with blinds. On the road outside the house the parking spot was empty - caught in a square of stray sunlight.

She went around to the garden to wait for Steele.

When she lifted the latch and walked through the door, she saw with a shock that Summer had gone. The greenhouse was stripped and bare. Outside its door rows of flower pots with pruned fuchsia and geraniums were stacked, ready to be stored away for the winter. The paths and small lawns were deep in russet leaves which were still falling damply from the tall sycamores surrounding the outside walls of the garden. The high stone walls were covered with ivy, here and there clumps of white daisies hung from fibrous roots. She wandered through the deserted garden and then sat, stoopbacked, on the rustic seat, listening to the morning rain still dripping from leaf to leaf. She was used to spending long hours alone and didn't notice how long she was there until she stirred from her thoughts and saw she had purple patches of cold on her legs. She was just beginning to stand up, stiff and cramped, when the door opened and Steele came in.

She made a move towards him and then stopped - alarmed by the change in his appearance. He came slowly towards her, almost shuffling along, his face puffy, his eyes swollen and red-rimmed. He was wearing a dark formal suit, a funeral suit. In the clear Autumn light his swarthy skin looked yellow and aged. He sat beside her and bent his head. She could see how sparse his hair was at the crown of his head.

"I heard about the baby. I'm sorry"

He turned towards her and nodded his thanks. Close to him she saw that the pupils of his eyes were huge and black and that he had the lost blind look of the very short-sighted.

"I knew you'd come down as soon as you heard."

He sat staring at his hands, twisting them backwards and forwards.

"What happened?"

How could his baby die? He was the medicine man, the healer.

He raised his shoulders and held his hands out.

"We won't know the cause until this evening, not officially. But of course we do know ... sometimes a plug of mucus can clog the respiratory passages of an infant ... a doctor, a midwife, can easily clear it."

He seemed to have forgotten that he had once discussed a similar case with her.

"But surely in the hospital ..."

"She didn't get to the hospital, she stayed at home until it was too late ... waiting for me."

"And you were with me?"

"Yes."

They sat there silently, numbed by the knowledge of their shared guilt. After a while, Kate said, "Was she all alone? Is she ...?"

"She's fine, physically. Lizzie Trodden was there, fortunately she came back to do something or other. She did all she could."

Then he clamped his shaking hands together.

"It was a boy, you know."

"She'll have another baby."

He shook his head.

"This was the miracle baby."

Kate thought of Mrs Steele forever arranging flowers for the hall table, weaving tapestry, knitting egg-cup covers.

She had no words to comfort him, no experience to draw on. For the first time in her life she was totally unselfconscious, almost unaware of her actions and moved by a deep love and pity for his pain and bewilderment she reached towards him, put her arms around him and drew his head to her breast. She could feel his body relax in her arms, she saw the tension leave his face, he closed his eyes. He had always been so strong, so full of energy and vitality, he had buoyed her up when she was low, today he was deeply wounded and for a while he was off guard, weak and vulnerable - hers to hold and comfort. She bent to kiss his face and her lips were salt wet with his tears.

She felt his arms tighten around her waist, then slowly he straightened up until they were facing each other. The air around them was strange and still - suddenly the birds had ceased to sing. For a moment he leaned so close that their breaths mingled, his lips almost touching hers, then he drew back.

"I have to go." His voice was hoarse. He stood up and looked away from her. "I have to make arrangements at the hospital, visit my wife. I can drop you off if you like."

She shook her head looking at the ground.

"No, I'll stay here for a while."

"Don't stay too long. Do you see how dark the sky is? It'll rain."

Rain, she thought, what do I care about it.

As the door closed behind him a large drop fell from the sky and rolled down her cheek like a tear. Another drop splodged onto the back of her neck and trickled coldly down her spine. She sat stoically on the rustic seat and let the rain pour over her, wash her clean. It pattered on the ivy and drummed on the roof of the greenhouse. Small rivers streaked through the clay path and filled into muddy pools. Her toes slid around in mucky sandals.

When the first flash of lightning came, it lit up the dark garden and brought her quickly to her feet. She ran in blind panic to the greenhouse. Another flash of lightning sprang from deep in the heavens. Thunder rattled the glass of the greenhouse and rain battered its door beating her into the open. She ran sobbing with terror and whimpered along the paths in the driving rain. As the lightning crackled overhead she reached the toolshed at the bottom of the garden and, slipping and sliding through a puddle of bouncing hail, fell blindly through it. She banged the door shut and moved into a corner. She breathed damp and mould and new-mown grass from the mower beside her. For the moment she was safe. The door was roughly made, too small for the frame. Through a gap she could watch with terror and excitement as lightning ripped across the sky - fiery fingers of God seeking her out for retribution.

Her mind was numb with guilt. She had been told by a priest that she must never see this man again. She had promised God through him and she had broken her promise. Twice she had broken it, had held this man in her arms and told him that she loved him. She had always thought of God as kind and understanding. She closed her eyes and tried to explain that she had never felt this way about any human being, to bear with her and she would go away as soon as she could, but the only image she could conjure up in her mind was that of Fr McGlinchey with his crewcut hair and small suspicious eyes. She slid down in a corner, her arms hugging her knees, her head bowed.

Outside there was a footstep, she lifted her head to see a shadow appear at the bottom of the door. Then the door was pushed roughly open and Steele came in, his dark suit covered in hail.

"Merciful God, Kate, what are you doing down there? Look at the state of you, you're drenched to the skin." He pulled her to her feet and began to dry her hair roughly with a handkerchief he pulled from his pocket. He chided her like an anxious mother.

"You'll catch your end in those clothes ... what sort

of an eejit are you that you came out without a coat ...
do I have to watch you all the time!"

Kate didn't care how much he gave out to her. With
his arrival, normality returned, her feelings of guilt
and remorse were pushed into the background. But
she was shivering uncontrollably, her teeth were
chattering.

"I should bring you straight home but you can't go
out in that storm."

They could hear the wind whistle around the shed.

He opened his jacket.

"Put your arms around my waist, here like this.
Don't be shy, I won't bite you. I'll wrap my coat
around you and the heat of my body will keep you
warm - it's an old survival technique."

She stood with her back to the stone wall of the
shed, her arms clasped tightly around his waist. She
could feel the steady thump of his heart, beating
strongly, warming both of them.

"I was on my way to the hospital when the
lightning came, I knew that if you were still here
you'd be terrified ... I had to see if you were alright."

"How did you know I was afraid of thunder."

Close against him she could feel his warm breath
on her hair as he laughed. "You had to be afraid of
thunder."

He squeezed her to him, she lifted her arms and
clasped them around his neck. Just at that moment a
gust of wind blew the door of the shed wide to the
wall. Lizzie Trodden was standing right outside the
door. She was staring at them. Her mouth had fallen
open with shock and horror. The eyes that turned on
Kate were flaming with hatred. Then with immense
control she turned to Steele.

"There was a message for you on the telephone. You are required to be at the hospital for five-thirty this evening." Then she turned on her heel and walked back towards the gate.

And every line of her retreating figure spoke of outrage.

Chapter Seven

Over cups of tea and wholemeal scones, served in the room behind the lace curtains Lizzie Trodden passed her information to key cronies and waited with satisfaction until it had filtered through to every level of the street. Anybody who transgressed against the high moral standards of King Street had to be punished and Kate and Harriet were boycotted. Gradually heads turned away as Kate walked by, doors closed as Harriet walked along the street. In the little shop across the street Minnie Corr was always busy when Harriet went in to buy the few odd groceries that would save her a trip down the town that day. She would wait patiently at the empty counter while Minnie kept her back turned and dusted and tidied the dummy display boxes at the back of the shop. Then she would hobble over and serve her silently with none of her customary small talk and Harriet, sensitive in the extreme, would sense her hostility and return to the house puzzled and depressed.

Upstairs Kate roamed restlessly from the Protestant to the Catholic window watching the people passing by. Sometimes she would watch the young policemen of the Royal Ulster Constabulary pass by in pairs, coming and going from the new police station that was being built in the next street. Some of them were very handsome, she thought, squinting her eyes after them, seeing their dark green-tinged uniforms, their revolvers bulging in the holsters at their hips. But she would soon turn away without any real interest - to be handsome now one had to have a certain height, to have a certain colouring and be of a certain age.

On Sunday mornings she would watch a Christian family pass through the street going to their meeting house. The saved people, they were called in King Street and they were disliked more than the average Protestants. Probably because they were so different, Kate thought, watching their stately progress through the street. There were four in the family, a mother and father who carried large bibles and dressed in sombre clothes and two daughters who walked in front and who wore navy coats and thick black stockings. They never smiled or spoke to each other, nor did they glance right or left as they walked along. They didn't wear makeup nor have their hair cut and it was said in King Street they didn't cook dinner on a Sunday or light a fire in case they would break the

Sabbath. Is this the way my mother grew up, she would wonder because she knew Menary worshipped in the same hall as these people and this thought helped her to understand something of the finality of the step Harriet had taken when she had left this sect to marry a Catholic.

But downstairs Harriet had other things on her mind than thinking about her past. The night before a stone had been thrown and their sitting-room window was broken.

"Probably a crowd of drunks coming from the pub," Harriet said doubtfully when she had called Kate down and they were assessing the damage. Carefully she removed a few shards of glass from the lace curtains.

"I can't understand how we didn't hear anything."

"Send for the police," Kate said, white and shaking.

Harriet thought for a while, her finger on her lips.

"No, it wouldn't do us any good to have them calling here. I'll order a pane of glass from Brady's hardware and they'll fit it for me." She swept the glass up with a brush and pan and measured the window with an inchtape. The following morning she went down to the hardware shop early, the measurements carefully written on a piece of paper. We'll have to get it done immediately, I'm not looking at thone eyesore for a week."

Some time after Harriet went out, Kate heard the letterbox rattle and the faint whoosh of a letter gliding through the air. She opened the kitchen door and saw a large white envelope lying on the mat. She stepped towards it, her heart thumping. It was here at last. She opened it with trembling hands, saw the heading of the Royal Infirmary and read the opening lines.

Dear Miss Regan

We are pleased to inform you ...

Just as she started to read it, Harriet came through the door and dumped her basket of shopping on the round mahogany table. The table, weak at the centre pod tilted dangerously. She plumped down on a chair and ignored it.

"The basket," Kate shouted. "Quick, take it off or it will scrape the table."

Harriet sneered over the table.

"What odds if it does?"

Her lips began to tremble, she looked around the room with loathing. Kate looked at her in surprise. The table was polished twice a week and dusted every day. It was frequently examined for small scratches and rings.

"How I'd love to get away from this place, when I'm here the walls seem to be closing in on me. How did I end up here?"

It was a cry of despair.

Kate was reading and rereading the letter and was not paying much attention to what her mother was saying

"That oul' Trodden," Harriet went on. "I never did anything on her, I hardly know the woman. These are the hypocrites that are licking the altar rails, They don't know the meaning of Christianity."

Now Kate was listening. She watched her mother over the letter, feigning a casual interest.

"What did she do on you?"

"Do? I'll tell you what she did. I was scrubbing the front doorstep yesterday morning and I saw her and nodded over to her. 'Good morning' I said, as civil as you please. She got hold of her front door and slammed it in my face."

Kate felt nothing but relief.

"Thone one's an oul' oddity," she said. "I wouldn't let the likes of her worry me."

Harriet wasn't listening.

"This morning I came down King Street and there she was talking to a gang of her cronies. They were talking about me."

"How could they be, they know nothing about you."

"All their chatter stopped when I came near them. I gave them a civil 'Good morning' but they kept their backs turned to me and not one of them answered me. I could see Trodden's wicked oul' eye watching me."

Kate could see them now, their broad backsides encased in flowered wrap-around aprons, a solid wall of resentment against her. Harriet, she thought, was sensitive enough to recognise their animosity but she had no idea what they might be saying.

"I have tried so hard," she said, "but I don't fit in here with these people. They have never forgiven me for being a Protestant. Their religion is beautiful but I must live it my way. I could never burn a lamp in front of a holy picture, it would seem like idolatry."

Kate felt a pang of guilt. Harriet thought the women of the street hated her because of her former religion. Kate knew what Lizzie Trodden and her friends were saying as her mother passed by but she couldn't say. She changed the subject

"I've had a letter from the Royal Infirmary," she said. "I think they'll take me for the next training school in February. They've sent me a final form which must be signed by my doctor."

Her mother flushed with pleasure, forgetting her own troubles. She smiled and her face was beautiful.

"Well, that's good news, so your illness won't go against you after all. It was better to be honest on your application form. Now if the new school begins in February you'll have to get the form back to them as soon as possible. What day is today?" She thought for a moment. "You can go down to Dr Steele at two, he has an afternoon surgery."

"I'll leave it 'til four, he'll be finishing then."

* * *

The surgery was packed.

Patients spilled from the waiting-room into the hall. Kate stepped into the back of the queue and Maureen, the receptionist, came and locked the door behind her. She looked at Kate in surprise.

"You're a stranger."

Kate shrugged.

"I've been busy."

Maureen nodded back to the living quarters of the house.

"Him and her, they've been away for quite a while. Since she came out of hospital she hasn't been well at all ... seemed to have lost the will to live for a while. He was very concerned about her. They went off touring in France - it seems to have done her all the good in the world. We had a locum in but it's nice to have him back."

She leaned against the frame of the door and closed her eyes tiredly.

"I have to go home soon and leave him to it. I

haven't even had my dinner yet."

Kate moved slowly along to the end of the queue. Maureen came back and forward from the surgery to the waiting-room.

"Next please. Yes, come right on in."

Kate reached the waiting-room and squeezed in beside a large country woman who balanced a covered basket on her knee. Her slack body spilled onto the chair beside her.

"Excuse me please," Kate said.

The woman shifted reluctantly, scarcely budging, a token gesture. Kate teetered on the edge of her chair. The woman turned and thrust the basket towards her.

"Put that on the floor, daughter." She sat back, relaxing into the loose folds of her skin. The basket was light and a faint scratching came from its depths.

"Is it a kitten?"

She turned her dewlaps towards her.

"No, them's young chicks. Is it himself?" She nodded towards the wall nearest the surgery.

"Yes, he's just back from holiday. He's been touring in France."

"Good. Sometimes he has them oul' locals in. But I only go to himself. Them young fellas that's not married. What do they know about women's business?"

She clicked her false teeth in disapproval.

"Next please."

Maureen had left and Kate could hear Mrs Steele's cultured tones - now wishing the patients 'Good day' as they left - now speaking on the telephone. In the waiting-room men and women moved from one mahogany chair to the next, an introspective group, silently participating in some humourless game of musical chairs. The crowd dwindled. Steele had joined his wife in the hall. Kate couldn't see him but her spine responded with a shiver to the unexpected sound of his voice. Now she moved again and was facing the doorway into the hall, looking straight towards his back. He leaned over his wife's shoulder as they read a letter which she held in her hand. He pointed to something on the page and they both laughed. Just then the phone rang. Together their hands stretched towards it. Her hand reached it first. He walked away still smiling at some private joke they had shared.

"Next please."

He didn't look into the waiting-room as he passed.

The old woman stumbled to her feet and bent clumsily towards the basket. Her round haunches were inches from Kate's face.

"I'll mind your basket until you come out."

But she looked at her with suspicion.

"I'd as lief bring it with me."

Mrs Steele had disappeared.

Kate sat alone in the waiting-room.

Dinner smells wafted along the hall. Her stomach churned and rumbled. She punched it with her fist. Twenty minutes passed. At last the surgery door opened. The old woman trundled past, carrying her basket. Steele walked beside her, his arm around her shoulder.

"Now Mary Ellen, it's no wonder your kidneys have seized up. I told you not to leave off your red flannel petticoat."

Kate heard a loud slap and a squeal of delight.

"Keep taking the bottle and I guarantee you'll be

running night and day within a week. I'll see you on
Friday."

He was still laughing when he leaned around the
door.

"Next please."

His eyes widened in surprise.

"It's you."

He walked quickly before her towards the surgery.
Kate, walking hesitantly behind him, thought she saw
him look furtively down the corridor towards the
kitchen. He ushered her quickly into the surgery and
closed the door behind her. He seated himself at his
desk and began to write rapidly. Without looking up
he motioned her to a seat. This is unreal, thought
Kate, we are in a play, him and me. Soon we'll be
called to speak our words, act out our roles. But what
those roles were and what they would say to each
other she did not yet know. She waited patiently as
he continued to write, then he sat back.

"Can I help you?"

His voice was cold and distant, a busy doctor
visited by a neurotic woman who had developed a
crush on him. She passed her form over.

"I need to have this form filled in by you before I
can be accepted for nursing in England."

A nerve twitched somewhere near his eye. He took
the form from her, read through it and began to fill it
up rapidly.

"They've already written to me." he said "I
answered the letter yesterday. But I'll fill this up."

"You have to weigh me and measure me."

Touch me, love me.

"I know your height and your weight."

There was a photograph on his desk in a silver

frame. It was an enlarged snapshot of a young girl. It had been taken in summertime, Kate thought. She could see that the girl was squinting against the sun and that she had a smattering of freckles across her nose. Who was she that he gave her photograph such prominence? Somebody he preferred to her obviously. She could feel her hands shake, she had an urge to swipe it from the top of his desk, smash it on the floor and grind the smirking face under her heel.

"I suppose she had to get all her teeth out as well," she said sneering at the picture. Her voice was hoarse with jealousy. He looked in puzzlement from Kate towards the picture and she saw his face soften. There was a silence. Then he said.

"No, they didn't take her teeth out. That's one thing they didn't do to her before she died."

"She's dead? I'm sorry."

But she was not sorry. The dead girl was enshrined forever in his memory, young and tragic, not hard and cynical like her. She stood up and walked to the window.

She could see past the yard of his house, to the outhouses and behind them the tips of the tall trees that surrounded the garden. The branches of the trees seemed black and bare but even as she looked a ray of sunlight burst through the clouds and highlighted their greening tips.

Steele came over and handed her the form sealed in an envelope. He stood at her shoulder as she continued to stare through the window.

"When are you leaving?"

"The next preliminary training school begins in February."

After a silence he said.

"What about your mother? How does she feel about being left behind?"

Kate shrugged and said nothing. My mother, she thought, she didn't like to admit that she had never thought of asking her.

"I can't sleep," she said.

"Neither can I."

She turned around in surprise and caught his unguarded face. She was stunned by the pain in his eyes. He's suffering too, she thought. Their eyes met. Their glances searched and held. Just one step and he's mine. But she could not take that step, she must never tempt the wrath of God again.

"Kate, I want to say something, to explain." He walked away from her and stood facing the window.

"I thought I was safe, I thought I was protected by my age and experience, by the fact that I was married. God, we had everything to divide us. I just want you to know I went into this situation as innocently as you did."

He stepped close to her. He raised both his hands and gently his fingers traced the contours of her face. As always when she was near him she longed to reach out and touch him but she kept her hands rigidly by her side.

"Kate, you are young and strong. How I envy you. You have a chance to live your life away from this place. You need never be warped by prejudice and bigotry. Unfortunately, it's young people like you who leave an environment like this."

"You could leave too."

Sudden hope made her heart beat fast.

He dropped his hand from her face and stepped back from her.

"I'm an old boy - kicking the heels of forty. When you're my age, darling, I'll be pushing up the daisies."

With his back to the light from the window she couldn't see the expression on his face.

"Some day it will amuse you to think that you ever loved someone like me."

You are so wrong, she thought. I am what you have formed. Your ideas are now mine, your prejudices are mine, you are ingrained in my being. My taste in men is set forever.

"When you think of me in the future don't be too harsh in your judgement of me."

"I will never judge you."

"You will," he said. "You'll have to come to terms with this sometime."

She turned away from him and walked across the surgery to the door. It was the longest journey she had ever taken.

"You'll come down to see me before you leave? This is not goodbye."

She stood with her hand on the handle of the door and looked back at him, a man in early middle age, dwarfed by a tall Georgian window.

"Of course it isn't. You know I wouldn't go away without seeing you again."

But even as she said it she knew that she was lying.

* * *

They sat on the edge of the leather chair at each side of the old stove and looked at the tin trunk in the centre of the floor.

"But bright orange" Kate said to her mother. "Who painted it that colour? Your father?"

244

"I don't know," Harriet laughed. "It was in the attic at home for as long as I remember."

"Did you bring it with you when you went to England?" Kate asked, sensing a chink in her mother's armour.

She had always imagined a stealthy flight, ropes, windows, two young people running through the night. The trunk in the middle of the room was incongruously solid, proclaiming a different story. But she was not to hear it. She had gone too far. The eyes which had been laughing across at her dropped to the floor.

"The taxi should be here any minute," Harriet said. "It's not like Mr Gallagher to be late."

They sipped tea daintily from china cups and nibbled biscuits from a doily-covered plate. Harriet coughed.

"There are some things that you should know before you go to England."

"Like what?"

"Well, about boys and things like that."

"We learned all that at school, the nuns taught us," Kate babbled at her panic-stricken.

"Oh, did they really?" Harriet looked relieved. "It's just that you're only eighteen and with the time that you spent in bed you've had no experience in going out with boys." She smiled shyly at Kate. "Here you are going off to a foreign country and I know that you have never kissed a boy ... never been in love."

They both stared at the plate of biscuits. They had become the most important thing in the room.

"You know that you should never arrange biscuits on a plate," Harriet said. "It's bad form."

There was a rattle at the letterbox and they stood

up with relief. Harriet went to the mirror and put her hat on. She tilted the brim carefully. One eye disappeared. She pulled on her leather gloves and examined her hands back and front.

"My mother used to say that a French woman puts her gloves on in the bedroom, an English woman in the hall and an Irish woman in the street."

"Will I call Mr Gallagher to carry the trunk out?"

"No, help me with it. I don't want him coming in."

They lifted the tin trunk and carried it coffin-like through the hall. Mr Gallagher ran over and took it from them.

"You should have called me. This is not a job for ladies."

"So you're off to the Nursing?" he said as they drove off. "It's a shame to see all the wee Catholic girls leave their own country because there's no work for them. Them'uns up in Stormont know how to look after their own."

Kate felt her mother stiffen with disapproval. She gave a polite distant smile towards his back, then turned and stared through the window. He stopped suddenly. He's remembered that we're neither fish nor fowl, thought Kate. They turned out of King Street and drove down the steep hill towards the town. As they slid forward in the seat Harriet clung to the handstrap over her head. She nodded to Kate to do the same. She knocked her hat with her arm, tilting it to a rakish angle. Close to her, Kate could see that her lipstick was crooked. She knew that she had put it on furtively in her darkened room and couldn't see that the cupid's bow on one side was slightly higher than the other.

They turned into the main street and moved slowly

in the line of traffic. She looked out trying to memorise every detail of the town. Even then she guessed how much she would need it. Where the street narrowed to a bottle-neck the car slowed down and stopped. The driver sat at the wheel, a lined patient man with a shock of white hair. Kate had often sat in the same spot with Steele, watching him grow more and more impatient, drumming his fingers on the wheel and cursing eloquently under his breath.

"We can go the other way and cut out the town," he turned to Harriet. "If we stay in this traffic, this wee girl might miss her train."

He turned suddenly into the street where Steele lived. They came down slowly past the house. She looked for his car to see if he was home and saw it in the row of orderly cars neat in their parking spots, askew, at a crazy angle, where he had pulled up in a hurry and dashed into the house. The front door was closed.

If this were a film, she thought, the door would open as I passed. Steele would come out unexpectedly, drawn by telepathy and look straight into my eyes. And even as she looked the door opened, she watched breathlessly and saw Lizzie Trodden come out carrying a tin of Brasso and a cloth. She cast an evil look around the street and began to polish Steele's brass nameplate, while a dog peed fitfully behind her, watching her with malevolent glee through the Georgian railings.

"Stop gawking," said Harriet as Kate craned her head for a last look.

"Really." She looked at her daughter with outrage.

They reached the station. Mr Gallagher preceded

them onto the platform carrying the trunk shoulder high. He placed it at their feet and signalled to Harriet that he would wait for her outside. A porter came and removed the trunk. He stacked it with the other luggage at the edge of the platform, ready to store on the train. Kate saw that it glowed among the other baggage - embarrassingly hers.

"Well, there's no danger that you'll lose it," said Harriet, laughing again when she saw it. She looked at her gloves and pressed the leather down between her fingers.

"My mother always wore kid gloves," she said. "She used to say that you could always tell a lady by the gloves she wore."

"I'll write as soon as I arrive," Kate said. "When I settle down I might be able to get a flat. You could come over and live with me."

"That would be marvellous. I wouldn't mind shaking the dust of King street off my feet for ever. It would be lovely to live in England again."

She spoke without conviction. They both knew that Kate would never ask her and even if she did, Harriet would never come.

"What will you do now?"

"Oh, I'll keep busy," she said. "Thone oul' house takes hours to clean."

"I don't have to go. I could get something here." Kate blurted it out. She hadn't meant to say it. But Harriet's eyes slid away from hers and the glass was back.

"There's nothing here. You'll get a good training over there. You'll have something to fall back on in the future. You never know how things turn out in life."

The train appeared suddenly, screeching towards them. It chugged past them and stopped. Kate's heart began to beat with excitement. She could hardly breathe.

"Goodbye." Harriet held her hand out.

Kate took her hand and on an impulse leaned forward to kiss her. Even before her lips touched her face she knew that she had made a mistake. Harriet's eyes looked frightened but she held her face obediently towards her daughter, like a child who has to submit to a kiss from an old aunt with a wart and whiskers. She could feel her mother's body recoil, her gloved hand go limp, her skin shrink with revulsion as young lips touched cold cheek.

Kate dropped her hand.

She climbed onto the train and slid the window down on its thick leather strap. Harriet stood smiling up at her, the smartest woman on the platform. But Kate's eyes looked past her to the door where the ticket collector stood. Even now Steele could dash into the station and rush towards the train, reaching a bunch of flowers towards her. It was quite commonplace in films. A whistle blew, the train slid away from the platform. But even though she stood at the window until the station grew small in the distance the only figure still standing there was her mother. Then just as she began to feel ridiculous waving at the diminutive figure, the train gathered speed, swerved around a corner and she was gone. The churches stayed with her longer. They jutted arrogantly from the green fields vying for dominance, they thrust themselves towards the sky and towered over the speeding train, then they too began to recede, disappearing behind trees and hills, reappearing suddenly but more distantly until at last they shrank and finally vanished.

And they too remained only in memory.

THE END

Attic Press Fiction

Mary Ryan
Whispers in the Wind
A richly satisfying saga of love and intrigue set in Ireland during the turbulent years of the early 1920s.
ISBN 1 85594 001 9   £4.99 / $9.99

Linda Cullen
The Kiss
The sensuous and troubling story of two young women whose childhood friendship turns into an intense and sexually explosive passion.
ISBN 1 85594 002 7   £5.99

Mary Rose Callaghan
The Awkward Girl
"A determinedly realistic Irish feminist novel." *The Irish Times*
ISBN 0 946211 957   £5.95 / $11.95

Eilís Ní Dhuibhne
The Bray House
"Highly recommended." *First Edition, RTE*
ISBN 0 946211 965   £5.95 / $11.95

Paula Martinac (Editor)
The One You Call Sister
"[These stories] cover the spectrum of sister relationships from closeness and shared secrets to envy and resentment." *The Irish Times*
ISBN 0 946211 116   £5.95

Ronit Lentin
Night Train to Mother
"An absorbing, satisfying book." *The Irish Times*
ISBN 0 946211 809   £12.95 (hb)
ISBN 0 946211 728   £5.95 / $11.95 (pb)

Leland Bardwell
There We Have Been
"Most economical and compelling." *Sunday Tribune*
ISBN 0 946211 817   £3.95 / $7.95

Leland Bardwell
Different Kinds of Love (Short Stories)
ISBN 0 946211 353   £9.95 (hb)
ISBN 0 946211 345   £3.95 / $7.95 (pb)

Eilís Ní Dhuibhne
Blood and Water (Short Stories)
"An impressive debut." *San Francisco Chronicle*
ISBN 0 946211 531   £12.95 (hb)
ISBN 0 946211 54X   £4.95 / $9.95 (pb)

Evelyn Conlon
Stars in the Daytime
"She has a delightful wit: dry, rather sour, but very accurate."
ISBN 0 946211 787   £4.95

Evelyn Conlon
My Head is Opening (Short Stories)
ISBN 0 946211 337   £9.95 (hb)
ISBN 0 946211 329   £3.95 / $7.95 (pb)

Melissa Murray
Changelings (Short Stories)
ISBN 0 946211 426   £12.95 (hb)
ISBN 0 946211 418   £4.95 / $9.95 (pb)

Ailbhe Smyth (Editor)
Wildish Things: An Anthology of New Irish Women's Writing
"Proof that we who read are in the midst of a revolution of the imagination." *The Irish Times*
ISBN 0 946211 744   £15.95 (hb)
ISBN 0 946211 736   £7.95 / $15.95 (pb)